MW01136234

THE ESSENCE

OF BETRAYAL

By
RJ Buchanan

Copyright © 2015 Ralph Buchanan

All rights reserved. No part of this publication may be reproduced, distributed, or transmitted in any form or by any means, including photocopying, recording, or other electronic or mechanical methods, without the prior written permission of the publisher, except in the case of brief quotations embodied in critical reviews and certain other noncommercial uses permitted by copyright law. For permission requests, write to the publisher, addressed "Attention: Permissions Coordinator," at the address below.

IVP
Publishers Desk
6547 Ann Arbor Road
Jackson, MI 49201

PART ONE

All events come in threes:
Good events, bad events and curses.
Fate won't be deterred.

Chapter 1

Jason waited patiently under the front porch of the fishing cabin. He hated to wait but tonight he had no choice. Tonight he had to do his father's bidding. His father protected him and gave him advice.

His thoughts drifted to the day his father discovered his stash of polaroids. There had only been three victims then (there were many more now) but his father was irate just the same.

However, his father had understood when Jason explained that they were just whores and that made it okay. Still his father insisted that he move off the ranch. Father bought him the old farmhouse – with no neighbors – so he could have his fun and no one would hear the screams.

Jason liked it when they screamed.

He felt himself stir when long last the porch light clicked on. The wait was nearly over. He felt the rush of anticipation spread through him. He had worried that it wouldn't be the same this time because he hadn't selected Martha. She was pretty though, if a little older than he liked them. Most importantly she was a whore, and this one was for his father.

Jason watched Warren through the cracks between the planks as he crossed the porch and descended the front steps. He knew Warren would leave first. Warren always left first, Martha stayed behind to shower and tidy up. At least that's how it happened the last two Saturday nights. Jason knew because he had been in this exact spot on those occasions, but his father had forbade him to do anything more than observe.

Jason watched Warren back out the drive and pull down the dirt road that circled Lake Parish. Five minutes after Warren's taillights had faded out of sight, Jason wiggled his way silently out from under the porch. His heart began to thump like it always did when he was closing in on the prey. The planks of the porch groaned slightly at his passage, but he was far too engrossed in the moment to notice. When he reached the front door he went stock still and listened. Nothing but the crickets made a sound. Martha, he reasoned in his demented mind, must be in the bathroom at the back of the cabin. He knew the floor plan of the cabin all too well. He had spent many weekends here with his father as a boy and though it had been some years since he'd been inside, the layout of the cabin was etched in his mind.

He paused at the bathroom door. Listening, he could hear Martha stirring about on the other side. He grew painfully erect and closed his right hand around the antler handle of the hunting knife at his waist. The blade whispered against the sheath as he pulled the knife free. He drew a deep breath through his nose and found the doorknob with his left hand.

She's going to scream, he thought. A demonic smirk curled on his lips, expectation surged through his twisted mind.

Jason loved it when they screamed.

Jason flung the door wide.

Martha screamed...

Jason paused only a second to enjoy the terror of her scream. Then with two quick strides he crossed the bathroom and backhanded Martha to the floor. "Shut up whore! Or I'll kill you now," he said with a rib crushing kick that slid the disoriented woman crashing against the bathtub, gasping for breath. With Martha dazed, withering in pain, Jason took a moment to savor the prize balled up in a fetal position before him. She wants me, he thought, just look at the way she's pulled up her robe to show me her lacy panties. He knew it, just another whore.

"Jason, why?"

"Shut up whore!" He stomped her head against the porcelain tub before he could stop himself. He had learned a lot since his first time. You had to control yourself because if you got carried away than they wouldn't wiggle when you gave them what they wanted. He liked when they wiggled.

Martha moaned and began to regain consciousness.

"You don't have to beg whore." He smiled wickedly as he open her robe. "I'll give you what you want."

~ ~ ~

An almost constant breeze pushed the unusual chill of the May night through the dense stand of live oaks and scrub brush.

A man checked his watch for the third time in as many minutes.

"Almost nine", he thought, "not long now."

From his vantage point he could see approximately a mile of the desolate country road before it twisted out of sight. There could be no more perfect location for his plan to be carried out. Even with its evil intent, or maybe because of it, the plan was beautiful.

But then a plan was like a chain; its true strength is measured by its weakest link. He silently willed David the strength to carry out his part.

In the distant darkness the amber sharpness of headlights sliced through the night like a razor through rice paper. His heart rate doubled and hammered its exhaustive tempo in his ears. Was this the one? The car for which he waited? Questions flashed through his mind like a strobe light.

The car approached at what seemed an unusual rate. It was close now, he tried to focus. Closer, he held his breath in anticipation. Closer, almost to him... No! Wrong car. He expelled the breath, burning his lungs with a whoosh!

Again he waited, forcing himself to relax. Breathe, he coached himself. In through the nose, out through the mouth, breathe. Be patient.

Like deja vu a second set of lights appeared in the inky blackness. This time the lights were accompanied by driving sound of an engine. He waited. FOCUSED. Took a deep breath and held it.

Yes! That's the one! He nearly screamed it to the night. He fumbled with his two-way radio. "Dave," he whispered, keying the mic. "That's our man. Stand-by. Copy?"

"Copy, James," came David's metallic voice through the radio.

James started the motorcycle and darted out of the stand of trees. Careful not to close too quickly he brought the motorcycle up to speed. Just as he topped a slight rise in the road, the pursued man's car crossed a bridge at the foot of the hill. Any moment now, he thought, pleading in his mind 'Dave please do your part.' As if David heard his plea the road in front of the marked man's car exploded in a flash of flame. The engine of James motorcycle raced almost of its own accord, closing the distance between itself and the hunted man at neck breaking speed.

James watched the pursued man's taillights sway left; snap right, swing back to the left, then with a lurch the car slammed hard into the ditch. So far so good, he thought. The gasoline had worked just as planned.

David had poured 5 gallons of gas on the asphalt road and ignited it just ahead of the man's car. David had come through for James. Now, all that remained was for James to finish the job.

James flashed through the dying flames, now, no more than a few inches high. He stopped behind the wreck. Its fenders and hood, shoved back and wrinkled, were sputtering and smoking from gapping seems. He could see the driver slumped over the steering wheel, motionless.

Looking back at the road he saw David scramble over the guardrail and check both directions to make sure they were alone.

The moment of truth had arrived. James leapt into the ditch a few feet from the driver's window. He could see blood streaming from Warren's forehead — dark streams flowing over alabaster skin. A moan from the wounded man coupled with a slight stirring refocused James to the situation at hand.

As if by magic the .38 special appeared in James' hand, becoming an extension of his arm. He watched his hand rise as if it belonged to someone else. Automatically his eye sighted his target a mere six feet from the end of the barrel. BOOM! BOOM! The second shot – sounding louder than the first rang in his ears as his eyes readjusted from the muzzle flash.

~ ~ ~

Jason pulled Martha's car to a stop on the phosphate mine access road that started on the ninety degree turn where Jameson Road turned into Walter Hunter Road. He killed the lights and climbed from the automobile taking a scarce moment to study the night sky. The stars were crystal clear in the absolute darkness of the secluded country road. It was a beautiful night and more so because, at least for the moment, his consuming hunger was sedated.

Back to the task at hand, Jason opened the back door of the sedan and dragged Martha's lifeless, robe clad body from the back seat. Painstakingly he adjusted her body into a provocative position so the first motorist that passed would find her exposed and wanton in her eternal state of repose.

After admiring his handiwork Jason returned to the car for his bag of gear. Although his father had strictly forbade it, Jason pulled his Polaroid camera from the bag and snapped several photos at different angles. For Jason this part was nearly as intoxicating as the act itself. He felt the same buzzing in his brain, the same quickness of breath.

Placing his treasures in the bag he removed a flashlight and towel. Dropping to hands and knees he wiped all his boot prints from the soft topsoil of the dirt road. That done, he jogged down the hill to the bridge where earlier that evening he had stashed a dirt bike. With a quick kick the 250cc motor roared to life and with the practiced ease of a lifelong rider Jason headed up the small stream away from the road.

A few minutes later Jason turned from the bank of the creek across a small meadow and climbed a dike positioning himself at an angle where he could witness the discovery of Martha's body. This was to be a new experience for Jason. He had never witnessed the discovery of his handiwork before. As he waited, the exhilaration of anticipation surged through him. He knew his wait would not be too long. Although this was a rural passage, it was only a couple miles from Lillie Bridge, a favorite party spot of local young adults and teens.

It had been his father's idea to dump his stepmother's body here where it would be quickly found. He normally dumped his victims in the swamp or on mine land. A few had been found but many had yet to be discovered.

Jason had been waiting for over an hour or so when he saw the headlights climbing the hill that led up from Lillie Bridge. The exhilaration that had started to fade reinstated itself and grew to mammoth proportions. His wait was over. The time had come.

Jason watched as the approaching car slowed to take the sharp curve. He heard the brakes lock. Saw the car reverse quickly. A few seconds passed or maybe a minute – he couldn't tell in his heightened state – then the car raced away.

Jason clicked the light button on his watch and checked the time. The Hillsborough County Sheriff's office would be responding to this call and he wondered what their response time would be. He knew he shouldn't wait but he couldn't force himself to leave. He was enjoying himself too much.

He searched the night in both directions of the approaching road for the red and blue flashing lights that he knew would come.

When at last they appeared in the distance he pushed himself to his feet. The deed was done. He kicked the motorcycle to life and rode off into the silent night.

~ ~ ~

Anger, misery – was there no end to this? What of this newfound power he felt churning inside him, intensifying the old anger, misery, and loneliness?

The first orange-yellow rays of the morning sun cast the room into purple-violet shadows. Sleep had eluded him throughout the seemingly endless night. James had lain, as motionless as death itself, for hours in the darkness. Torment gripped his tortured drug addled mind.

Urgent pounding rang out in the stillness of the peaceful morning. Terror roared through him as he rolled to the floor; the .38 caliber still firmly in his grip. He swore to himself they would never take him alive. Sweat stung his eyes as he scooted his back against the wall and aimed his pistol at the closed door. He heard the front door swing open, then the careful slow steps of someone walking down the hallway towards the room. How could the police know? It had to be a setup. Well, they would get the surprise of a lifetime! Head shots, he told himself – cops wore bulletproof vests.

The sound of steps stopped outside the door. Should he just open fire? He sat in silent debate, his trembling hands sweaty and tense. Aim high; aim real fucking high. He pulled the slack out of the trigger and thumbed back the hammer. With an eerie click it locked.

"James, are you awake?"

David's voice broke through his delusional mind as he released the breath he hadn't realized he was holding. "Yeah, I'm awake." James lowered the handgun as the bedroom door swung open.

"What the fuck, man? Have you completely lost your mind?" David was stunned at his best friend's condition and his voice rang with contempt. "What exactly are you doing?"

At that moment James realized how stupid he must look, "I thought... Thought you...", he stammered. "The po - lice..." James drew a much-needed composing breath. "The way you came busting in here. What's so Hells fire important to get you chargin' in here like you got a pack of wild dogs hot on your ass?"

David threw the Sunday paper on the floor at James' feet.

"Look for yourself."

The bold black print scrawled across the top of the newspaper read: "Prominent Businessman's Wife Latest Victim of Rural Rapist "James stumbled into the kitchen where David sat at the table. "Who is it then?"

"How the fuck should I know," David shot his answer out in anger and frustration.

"You know this means we killed an innocent man last night."

"Don't remind me."

"How can you ever forget that?" James asked.

"I won't. What do we do now?" David said, the weight of their actions heavy in his tone.

"We figure this out and avenge Warren's death since he can't, thank us."

"Boy, Dante played us like a piano, showing us all those pictures, telling us he found them in Warren's bedroom..." David shook his head in disbelief at their naïveté.

"It has to be someone close to Dante," James said, walking to the kitchen counter. "Or how could he have all those crime scene Polaroids to show us in the first place?"

"Yeah, you're right."

"Of course I am." James dropped a ball of cotton in the spoon he'd just mixed water and speed in. "Now all we have to do is find out who it is."

"How are we going to do that?"

"I wonder if..." James put the tip of the needle in the cotton and drew the solution into the syringe. "No, Dante wouldn't be so dumb to..." James pushed the needle into his arm. "Do you think Dante gave the recipe to the one that killed Martha?" James pushed the plunger down and felt the heat of the crystal-meth course through his veins.

"What difference would that make?" David asked after James recovered from the initial rush of the injected speed.

"Because they have to sell it and unless they do it elsewhere we'll know the minute it hits the street."

Chapter 2

Homicide detective Robert Mayhew stood at the edge of the rural road with his hands shoved deep in the pockets of his off-the-rack black suit-pants. He carefully surveyed the scene slowly twisting his head from side to side in disbelief. This, he mused, doesn't happen here; maybe up north in the upper Mid-West, back in the day when the mob was in their hay-day, but not here. For Christ sake, this was a peaceful Southern town and gangland style murders just didn't fit in this tranquil setting.

In his near 20 years on the force this was the most out of place crime scene he'd ever worked. This whole scene was wrong; the pieces just didn't fit. This case was going to change the rules, he had that feeling deep in his gut.

I'm getting too old for this shit, he thought. His mind drifted back to the Westhardt rape/murder scene he'd worked until well after midnight. A gruesome, senseless crime of a serial rape and murder, but this crime scene had an undertone of passion that far exceeded random acts of the rural rapist.

Maybe, he pondered, it's just me? He closed his eyes and massaged his temple. The image of a man on the backside of 40 swam into focus, the boyishly long hair graying at the temples in sharp contrast to itself. The face creased hard beyond its years and showing the weight gain, common of middle-age, was the face that looked back at him in the mirror this morning. He'd splashed water on his sagging, puffy face and studied the black bags that clearly announced his lack of sleep to anyone taking care to look into his eyes. But duty had called early; killers didn't punch a time clock. So here he stood, the sun just peeking over the trees on the distant eastern horizon, its May warmth doing little to temper the chill he felt in his weary bones.

"Mayhew," a crime tech called out.

"Yeah".

"We're finished here".

"What can you tell me?" Mayhew asked walking toward the edge of the bridge.

"Not much at the moment; I could speculate if you want."

"Let's hear it", Mayhew said, urging the tech to continue.

"Well", the tech replied. "It appears that the victim was traveling east when someone set the bridge on fire with gasoline. The victim swerved, locked up the brakes, lost control and wound up in the ditch. At that point the perpetrator fired two rounds into the victim's head at close range – maybe 10 feet – with what appears to have been a .38 caliber or 9 mm handgun."

"One perp"? Mayhew asked.

"We didn't find anything that would suggest otherwise."

"What about the time of death?"

"Eight, maybe 10 hours ago," the tech guessed.

Mayhew checked his watch – sometime between nine and midnight, he calculated. "When did we get the call?"

"5:30, 6 o'clock, I think. Some old man on his way to work called it in."

The tech nodded his understanding and left. Mayhew watched the tow truck hook the cable to the rear axle of the wrecked automobile and winch it onto the flat bed rollback truck. A few feet of skid-marks and tire ruts in the ditch were the only signs of foul-play that remained. The work at the scene was completed but Mayhew's work had just begun; a tiresome task and mystery that, try as he may, he may never find a solution for.

~ ~ ~

SIX DAYS LATER

"That's my point exactly; everyone has a price. You, me, the law – everyone." James stepped into the open door of the barn in search of some relief from the lingering chemical odors. "And it would do us good to learn to use that to our advantage. It may not always mean money... might be a service like we did for Dante or maybe drugs, but once we figure someone's price, we can bend them to our will."

"I don't know James. I don't like to use people," David interjected.

"Come on man, everybody uses everybody else. We're not talking about forcing anyone to do anything. We just offer to pay for their services, that's all." James ducked back into the dim interior of the barn. "Same as the way Dante used us. We sold our soul for the recipe to make this shit – why? Because the pot is getting harder to grow with all the new surveillance equipment the cops use. My daddy is probably rolling over in his grave at my recent actions, but times are changing. Hell, my granddad probably did some wiggling in his own grave when my daddy switched from bootlegging whiskey to growing reefer."

"The fact that the police killed your grandfather for bootlegging and your father for growing pot is something we should really consider. I mean hell, you were only 18 when you planted your first pot field. Now 10 years later we're cooking crystal-meth. When does it end?" David paused for effect. "When the cops kill you, that's when it fucking ends."

"Relax Dave, I've been drinking homemade whiskey since I was 10 and smoking pot since I was 12 and I know the cops killed my father and grandfather, but I don't intend to make the same mistakes they made. You see, they stayed in the game too long, because they couldn't make enough money to get ahead." James pointed at the freshly

[15]

manufactured crystal-meth. "But we can make a mint off this 'SHIT' and then we get out."

"You forgot one thing."

"What's that?"

"You've been shooting up crystal-meth since you were 15." David answered.

"Quit bustin' my balls." James said as he drew up the mixture of water and speed into the syringe. "And look at the bright side."

"What's that?"

"I no longer have to buy speed. Now I have an unlimited supply." James laughed as he pushed the needle into his arm.

The sound of a distant train vibrated in James ears. His eyes swam quickly out of focus as he struggled to draw breath that just wouldn't come. The injected speed raced through his veins forcing droplets of sweat out the pores of his skin. The droplets joined together and formed transparent rivulets that dripped to the floor. The rush chased away all conscious thought, leaving hyper intensive pleasure in its wake. Like a high-speed train the moments flashed by. Slowly the intensity subsided and the real world pushed its way back into his vision.

"Wow, what a rush!" James mopped the sweat from his forehead. "That may be the best speed I've ever done... I'll give Dante his props – that's one helluva recipe. That shit just rocked my world."

"I gather," David said, "from your reaction I can call Wes and set up the deal?"

"Damn right, set up the deal; we're rich! I don't know who his buyer is but whoever it is they're going to love this shit. And this well ain't runnin' dry—we have an endless supply. I just hope the buyer has long money."

When David scooped the phone from its cradle and started punching numbers James drifted off in thought. Two-hundred grand worth of meth lay before him in ziplock bags on the table. A new Corvette drove by in his mind's eye

[16]

with him at the wheel. Slowly, flauntingly, he drove the vette through town, basking in the looks of strangers as they stopped to stare as he passed. Crawling to a stop at a red light he called out to a pair of beauties on the sidewalk, *"Hello ladies: Want to take a ride in my machine?"*

"James you still here with me?"

The sound of David's voice brought James back from his dreams of easy street. "Yeah what'd Wes say?"

"We meet him tomorrow at his place. His people are ready; they been waiting on us... Some guy named Russo."

~ ~ ~

The backlit image of Wes's face appeared in the front window as James and David climbed from James' worn Camaro.

"It's Showtime Dave Ole' boy the moment of truth." The excitement palpable in James' voice as he ran his fingers along the sleek fender of the 520 Benz they had parked next to. "Look at her, ain't she a beauty Dave?"

The front door swung open at their approach. Wes's medium build appeared in the opening. His brownish hair framed his chiseled features, features softened by an easy smile. "Y'all got the shit?"

"Right here." James held a black canvas bag as he swaggered past Wes with David in tow. The lingering effects of the injected speed coupled with the excitement of the moment had his confidence at an all-time high. Never faltering, he made his way to the kitchen table, with an appraising look at the stranger seated there.

The stranger was of obvious Latin descent, dark eyes, and close cropped coal black hair lending a chilling air to his pockmarked face. But it was his dark eyes that most struck James: there was a darkness in those eyes.

No matter, James thought; get the money, then get the fuck outta here. Who really cared who this Russo guy was or what evil squirmed inside him?

[17]

"So, Russo." James never broke eye contact as he spoke. "I guess it's you I'm here to see?"

Russo's response came as a solemn head nod.

James hardly noticed when Wes and David joined him and the silent stranger at the table. Something about the stranger bothered James but he couldn't put a finger on his uneasiness. He pushed the thought into the recesses of his mind to study later. He regained his focus on the matter at hand. "Well, if no one objects..." James scanned the faces at the table. "Let's do this thing. – I've got ten pounds of uncut crystal. The price is one-hundred grand and it's damn well worth it. If y'all are interested let's see the color of your money." James settled his eyes on the stranger indicating the last statement was directed to him.

Russo produced a paper sack and placed it on the table.

Opening the offered sack James discovered ten rubber-banded bundles of hundred dollar bills. His heart raced. "I'll take your word on the count," he said tossing the canvas bag of meth on the table. James stood. "Russo – Wes; y'all give me a call when you want more."

James eyed the Benz one last time as he backed down the drive. "Weird dude," James announced. "He never said a word."

"Yeah," David said. "He makes my skin crawl."

"No matter Dave; we're rich." James patted the sack of money between them. "Count thirty grand, that's your cut. Oh, and you better start the next batch of speed ASAP. With Warren out of the picture and Dante stepping back. Leaving us his customers, we're going to need it. A lot of it."

~ ~ ~

Mayhew's desk appeared as if it had more years on it then he did. In the center of its scarred surface a steaming plastic mug of black coffee rested next to the report on one Warren Allison, a 32-year-old male. The fact that Warren Allison had been murdered wasn't news to detective Mayhew

– far from it. Nor was the cause of death – two . 38 caliber head-wounds. However, the fact that Mr. Warren Allison was employed by Westhardt Inc, put a perplexed wrinkle on Mayhew's face. Coincidence? He doubted it.

If his years on the force had taught him anything it was that coincidence just didn't happen. *'Well,'* he mused to himself *'I have my first break.'* He began to create the scenario in his mind: older man with a young wife and along comes a young stud. Older man gets jealous and both the wife and her young lover get themselves murdered on the same night. Pretty basic, but now the hard part rested on his shoulders – prove a double homicide against a respected citizen who obviously had help, and no doubt enough money and powerful friends to cause trouble for a lonely detective trying to do his job.

Mayhew rang the doorbell for the second time. He could hear the ringing echo through the cavernous interior of the modern style ranch house. The hewn rail skirting the planked veranda was a nice touch he thought, not to mention the carved red oak doors or the arched window boxes. The place was a symbol of wealth and prosperity, but even here, the harsh reality of common everyday problems like infidelity crept in and destroyed lives.

After ringing the bell again, he returned to his car, he had time to wait. He slid in behind the wheel and into the comfort of the vehicle's air conditioner. Early May and already the days were a blistering 90°. The temp was rising and with it the homicide rate.

For lack of anything better to do while he waited, he punched the tag number of the three vehicles parked in the drive into his onboard computer. The two trucks were registered to a *Dante Westhardt*, the third was a late model Mustang belonging to one *Jason Tess*; a white male of 28 years who weighed 190, stood six-foot one and had blonde hair.

An approaching black F350 pickup caught his attention and he climbed out of the Crown Victoria allowing a fresh thick wave of May heat to wash over him. Two men disembarked the Ford truck. One he recognized as Dante Westhardt and the other fit the description of Jason Tess that he'd just read.

"Afternoon Mr. Westhardt," Mayhew said in a tone of kindness that he didn't feel the man before him deserved.

"Detective," Dante spoke in a much cooler tone, "What do I owe this pleasure to"?

"Well," Mayhew began, "it seems that one of your employees was murdered on the same evening as your wife, at approximately the exact same time and I found it to be quite the coincidence. So, I decided to drive out here and see if you had any ideas as to what happened — like maybe you have an enemy or something?" Mayhew watched for a reaction but none was forthcoming.

"Enemies detective? Hmmm... I'm a wealthy man, so I suppose I have enemies, but I can't think of any that would gain anything by killing my ranch foreman - Warren."

"How long did Warren Allison work for you?"

"Hell, six, maybe seven years, I reckon." Dante produced a hanky and mopped the sweat from his brow. "I can check his W-2s for an exact date, if you like?"

"No, no," Mayhew said retracting the question, "that won't be necessary. Did Mr. Allison live on the ranch?" He inquired, quickly replacing the retracted question.

"Sure, down back in the guest house."

"Mind if I have a look at his quarters? Might help solve his murder." Mayhew shot the question in rapid-fire method used to confuse a questionee.

"Anything to help detective." Dante replied, unmoved by the tactic. "Jason show the officer to the guest house." Then, without another word, Dante Westhardt spun on his heel and disappeared through the carved, hardwood doors of the ranch house.

The guest house was true to form; hardwood floors were covered with braided throw rugs that depicted wild stallions running free, others locked in mortal battle over breeding rights of the herd mare. The furnishings were rustic heavy oak, polished to a high gloss. The overall feel of the place gave the impression of a freshly cleaned and polished museum and nothing like the bachelor pad it was said to be. Mayhew remembered his old bachelor apartment; stacks of beer cans and old pizza boxes, not to mention the piles of unwashed laundry. Maybe, he mused, maybe married life wasn't so bad. But he couldn't hold back the boyish smile at the long forgotten memories.

Mayhew moved about the room opening a drawer here and a cabinet there. Yet, nothing was out of place; everything was neat and tidy, too neat and tidy. The place as a whole bothered him. Just a hunch but, somehow it just didn't sit right with him. There were no answers here and by all indications someone had gone to great lengths to make sure of that.

Back in the blazing, midday sun with Jason Tess matching his stride Mayhew asked, "You work for Dante Westhardt?"

"Uh-huh," Jason answered with a grunt and confirming nod.

"How long?"

"About three years."

"Do the Westhardt's have a maid?"

"Hell, Mister I don't know. I'm just the hired help. You want answers, ask Dante," Jason sneered. "I reckon you can find your car? *You bein' a detective and all.*" Then with a chuckle at his own cleverness Jason strolled around a mammoth fountain in the center of the back walk and into the rear entrance of the huge homestead.

Once inside Jason strolled apprehensively over the slate marble floor toward Dante's study. His foot only touched the middle of the three steps descending into the den.

Dante stood at a bank of windows that overlooked the front drive, sipping a drink and studying the retreating taillights of Detective Mayhew's Crown Vic. After a time, he

[21]

gingerly ambled towards the fireplace and studied the painted portrait of his great grandfather, in his confederate attire.

"What'd you make of that?" Jason's voice startled Dante.

"Don't panic boy!" Dante ordered.

"I'm not panicking. But..."

"But what?" Dante spun in anger, spilling his drink in the rash process. "I'll tell you what – you keep your mouth shut and do what I tell you to do. You understand that?"

Jason stared at a spot on the floor 6 inches in front of his snakeskin boots. "Uh-Hu," he mumbled like a scolded child.

Chapter 3

The streets of Tampa seemed different somehow – brighter maybe – James wasn't sure, but he couldn't ever remember feeling more alive. He took a quick glance at the paper sack of money on the passenger seat. *Tonight would be a night to remember*, he thought.

The pink flash of the 'NUDE GIRLS' neon sign cast an exotic glow on the stack of money James had extracted from the paper sack. He ambled toward the front door of the club, stuffing the thick fold of bills into his pocket. The bouncer working the club door appeared to have an abundant supply of steroids, yet James doubted he'd ever had an original thought.

"Cover charge's 20 bucks," the steroid-stallion said in a voice much too high pitched for his bulk.

James retrieved the thick knot of bills from his pocket peeling off a hundred from the stack. "Keep the change Brutus."

"Thanks, but the name's George." The steroid enhanced man replied.

The club smelled of stale booze, dense smoke and feminine sweat, but no one seemed to notice. James made his way through a rowdy crowd to a stool at the edge of the stage. A bleach-blonde worked her way around the platform vibrating to the music as patrons' stuffed bills in her garter.

"Could I get you a drink, sir?"

James turned to the sultry voice to find a net-clad waitress with ample breasts and a seductive smile. "Seven and Seven," he responded. She flashed another quick smile and walked towards the bar, her ass cheeks jiggling to the cadence of her steps.

Movement in his peripheral vision brought his attention back to the bleach-blonde who – still gyrating on the stage – had worked her way to where James sat. Dropping to her knees before him she slowly laid back exposing the mound of her sex, moist and glistening under the powerful lights. Ever the sport, James slid a crisp hundred in the blonde's garter and was rewarded with a fresh wave of enthusiasm. The dancer kicked her feet over the platform edge and spread herself giving James a personal view of her sex. Then, as agile as a cat, she rolled to her stomach and crawled to the glimmering chrome pole at center stage. "Your drink, sir." The net-clad waitress had returned. Artfully she brushed her stiff nipples against his arm as she placed his drink on the counter.

Plucking free another hundred James pushed the bill under the netting of her jumpsuit, into her cleavage. "Keep the change honey, and keep the drinks coming."

James turned back to the stage in time to see the next dancer waltz out, shedding an article of clothing with each dance step. Yeah, he thought, this is living. He waved a C-note at the energetic dancer. Quickly she sauntered over to him turned and backed herself within a foot of his face and bent forward. He stroked her gently as he slid the offered bill under the sheer fabric of her panties. She wiggled against his fingers and danced away.

"Hi, big tipper. By a girl a drink?"

James glanced toward the voice to find the bleach-blonde standing next to him in a tight vest that forced a deep cleavage between her breasts and a micro skirt that fell far short of covering her. "Sure honey, you wanna get a table?" James knew the game and how it worked, but tonight was different. Tonight he had the money to rewrite the rules.

He followed her to a dark corner of the club. "What's your name honey?" He asked as he marveled at the fact, that in the land of the free, all you needed was money.

"Trish."

"What?" James asked, snapping out of his daze of thoughts.

"My name is Trish."

[24]

With that the small talk and the game began. They chatted, laughed and drank. The conversation was pointless, the laughs were a lie. She wanted his money and he wanted the price, her price.

Finally she announced. "I've got the next set, will you be here when I get back?"

"Sure honey. I'll see you after your set," he said slipping yet another hundred in the waist of her micro skirt.

"You keep tipping like that and you can see me whenever you want."

"I'm counting on that," he said almost to himself and to her back as she walked in a hip-swinging saunter to the backstage door.

When the music next changed Trish pranced out on stage, still wearing the same vest and skirt, but not for long. In a matter of an agonizingly slow seconds she was naked as the day she was born. Trish handled the crowd of blue-collar workers like the pro she was, presenting herself for their view and collecting their hard-earned money in exchange for a fantasy that, for most, would never come true.

Soon after her set was finished she rejoined him at his table. James was stunned by her appearance in a blouse and a denim skirt – her attire wasn't, by any means, conservative but it was far more modest than he expected, and he said as much.

"That was my last set," she explained. "I'm heading home."

"Is that an invitation?"

"More of a gift than an invitation," she said shyly, "Mr. Russo asked me to spend the evening with you."

James scanned the club for the Latin stranger who had never spoken a word to him, an uneasy feeling spreading through him. He found the Latin in the far corner of the club, when their eyes met the Latin gave a quick stern nod. James answered the gesture with a nod of his own.

Then with a casualness he didn't feel, he followed Trish to the door.

~ ~ ~

It was early and the stifling heat of the sun hadn't forced away the coolness of the night yet. It would, it always did, but it would take a couple more hours. James sat on a balcony high above the city. He loved this time of day, the freshness of morning. For the past hour he'd been looking over the pages of pictured ads in the local Auto Trader. Before this day was done he would have a much nicer ride than the aging Camaro.

Trish walked out on the balcony still wearing James' is silk shirt. She is a beauty he thought, as she sat down on his knee allowing the shirt to ride up her thigh. He felt himself stir.

"Morning," she said, around a sleepy smile.

"Morning." He laid his hand on her exposed thigh. "Sleep okay?"

"Like a rock. You can wear a girl out."

James considered her words, knowing that her type were prone to lie, but then she had seemed to have enjoyed herself and he certainly had found some satisfaction in the pleasures of her lithe body. "You want to spend a few days with me?" He asked on impulse, knowing it was a mistake.

Trish shifted her position until she was straddling his lap. "You really want me to?" She asked as he slipped his hungry fingers under her lacy panties and began to probe her taut depths.

"Yeah, honey," his response was thick with desire. "I was kinda thinking I'd like a few encore performances to last night."

She maneuvered to slide down on his now exposed manhood. "You can have a repeat performance now."

Chapter 4

"Where the hell have you been?" David shouted, faced tight and crimson and twisted in anger.

"You want an itemized list or will a general summary do?" James smirked, mocking David's anger.

"I'm serious James! You disappear for two weeks. Then you show up with some bimbo and a flashy Corvette like everything is hunky–fucking–dory."

"The car is none of your business, neither is the bimbo for that matter, and last time I checked, my father died before I was born. So I answer to no man – got it?" James leveled his icy gaze at David in an open challenge. "Now," he continued, "for the record I went to see an old friend in West Palm and he wants 15 pounds. He's prepared to pay fifteen thousand a pound – cash."

Trish couldn't hear the conversation, but she knew from their actions it was heated. James' anger was clear in his body language, but what she found most disconcerting was the fact that in the two weeks she'd known him this was the first time she'd seen him show any emotion. Although the past two weeks had been amazing she'd never seen his composure falter. He was fun, but always distant.

Slowly the memory of their first time together drifted back to her. They'd nearly covered the state – partied in clubs on South Beach, had sex on the beach in Fort Lauderdale, chartered a boat in Jacksonville and stopped in Orlando to meet Mickey Mouse. Yet the fact remained she couldn't have given a single bit of insight as to what made up the man she only knew as James.

"Alright I'll call Wes and make the arrangements for the party," David said.

"I'm not bull-shitting Dave; I want a live band, plenty of booze and invite everyone we know." James' eyes seemed to have brightened. "In the meantime give me 15 pounds and I'll handle the West Palm business." She saw David return with a canvas bag that he promptly handed to

[27]

James. The two men exchanged words again, but the earlier heat seem to have faded. However, from her vantage point – and experience with men – it was obvious that James instilled fear in his friend. She wondered at the basis of that fear. Maybe, she thought, it had to do with the nightmares that woke James in the small hours of the morning.

The second night she and James had spent together had been the worst. James had tossed and turned and mumbled unintelligible words until abruptly he jerked awake and sat bolt upright in bed, a sheen of sweat covering his torso and worried face. Trish had feigned sleep while James grabbed his cigarettes and stumbled to the balcony. She had watched the glow of his cigarette brighten and dull with each drag. How long he'd stayed on the balcony she couldn't say; sleep had found her and dragged her to a much more peaceful realm then the realm James spent his nights in. In the morning he offered no explanation and she'd expected none. Every third or fourth night since, he would visit that realm of torment. Although she didn't ask she couldn't help but wonder what demons lurked in that realm of torment waiting to ambush him when he closed his eyes.

~ ~ ~

The murky canal water ran parallel to the two-lane highway. Tall sawgrass crowded the canal bank opposite the highway and the only thing that flourished in this vast marshland were the reptiles that dominated the food chain. Alligators stalked anything they deemed large enough to curb their ravenous appetite and cottonmouth pit vipers ate everything too small to interest even the youngest gators. This desolate stretch of highway had almost, from its inception, been nicknamed 'Alligator Alley' and rightfully so, this domain belonging to the prehistoric lizards. The two-lane passage allowed travelers to trespass, unharmed for the most part, but any deviation from the paved route and the prehistoric beast enacted their own form of justice to the violator.

Along the confines of the highway James and Trish rode through the swampy landscape. They had spent the better part of the past three hours in silence, each content to consider the world outside and their thoughts.

"Why are we going back to West Palm?" Trish broke the trance-like silence. She'd been considering the question for quite some time, but she wasn't certain she wanted to know the answer. Of one thing she was certain; it had something to do with the canvas bag James had picked up from his friend.

"I have some business to take care of," James glanced at her, then back at the road. "Why do you ask?"

"No reason. You just seem so somber, I wondered why."

"Ah. I was thinking about my grandfather; I always do when I come this way."

"This road reminds you of your grandfather?" Trish asked puzzled. "Why?"

"My grandfather used this road to run moonshine and I grew up hearing tales of high-speed car chases and close calls that he had on this road." James paused as if considering something then continued. "He died before my father was born, and my father, true to the family curse, trafficked coke and weed on this highway. And true to the family curse, he too, died before I was born. My mother died giving birth to me and my father's mother raised me. She told me the stories of my father and grandfather and made me promise not to do the things they'd done. But she died a few years ago so..." He let the words hang a moment. "Here I am carrying on a family tradition."

"James you don't –"

He held up a finger to silence her. "You asked, so listen. However you look at it, it's a necessary evil. Men, at times, detach themselves from orthodox opinion of what's right and wrong and create their own laws and justice system to govern the world of illicit free enterprise. I've never been one to sugar-coat things; I call it like I see it.

[29]

Drugs are a nasty business; some win – some lose. At times you're forced to do things you may regret, but it's the nature of the business. But everyone has the freedom of choice and at some point I'm sure we will all pay for our choices."

~ ~ ~

"Yeah, I know where that's at. I'll be there in 30 minutes." James hung up the phone, unzipped the canvas bag, removed a handgun and tucked it into the waist of his jeans.

"Everything all right?" Trish asked, her voice doing a miserable job of concealing her anxiety at seeing the weapon.

"It's Showtime, honey!" He patted her playfully on the ass as he walked out the door. "Don't worry about me. The game is cruel, but it's fair. I won't be long."

Trish watched him stroll out the door of the suite and wondered if she was in over her head. At first she thought he was just another mark. A man that she would use up and spit out, but she doubted anyone who'd been around James for any length of time would consider him a mark. The revelation about his family had only convinced her that he had a death wish or more likely he'd come to terms with his mortality. Whatever, she had a job to do. She just had to be careful. James was smart, and a dangerous man to cross she had a feeling. But for the moment, she would enjoy the ride. At least he was attractive and fun...

She was still sitting on the bed when he returned. The uncontained fire in his ice blue eyes froze her breath in her chest. At first she wasn't sure what fueled the fires in his eyes, but he didn't keep her in suspense. He shoved her back on the bed and for the first time Trish noticed the canvas bag in his hand. Her memory flashed back to the handgun and fear streamed through her veins like ice water, but before she could plead for mercy he unzipped the bag and dumped its contents on her. Hundreds, fifties and twenties poured from the bag and covered her and the bed.

Straddling her, James roughly fondled her breast. Then with a sudden jerk he tore open her blouse. Her shock was so complete at the sight of the money and the wild look in his eyes that she couldn't resist his contagious desire. He worked the clasp between her breasts, releasing her bra, as she tore at the button and zipper of his jeans. With hands full of money he rubbed her breast until she freed his fully erect manhood and began stroking him. He tossed the money aside and pushed her skirt around her waist. Then he snatched off her panties and tossed them aside. In one fluid motion he plunged into her encompassing silky depths. She tore at the soft skin of his back with her fingernails, sharing her pleasure and her pain. Viciously he drove into her only to be stopped by the upward thrust of her hips. The fury of their erotic frenzy escalated them towards a frenetic plateau. At the zenith, their rhythm exploded into convulsing shutters of orgasm.

Exhausted, they collapsed and slept the sleep of the dead. James didn't dream.

~ ~ ~

The annoying cadence of his cell phone rousted James from his slumber. He fumbled around in the darkness for the 'ON' button. "Yeah" his voice sounded as though he had gravel in his throat.

"James?" David asked, unsure.

"Yeah."

"Hey, we've got a problem. Wes will take the 5 pounds we talked about, but he won't pay more than thirty-five grand.

"What the fuck is Wes trying to pull!" James sat up in bed fully awake. Trish stirred beside him.

"Wes said he can get the same shit for seven thousand a pound someplace else."

"You understand what this means, right?" James shook his head in disgust, anger twisting his features.

"I think I do, but give me your take anyway."

"My take?" James added to harshly. "My take is simple. A person with dope like ours has the same recipe we do and logic says that person is the Rural Rapist."

"We don't know that for sure," David replied.

"Don't kid yourself. Dante had all those pictures of the crime scene. We got our recipe from him and now someone else has the same recipe. That's too much coincidence in my book."

"What are we going to do?"

"Not we Dave, me. I'll handle this; just don't mention it to anyone."

"Of course not."

"I'll be in Pinecrest this afternoon."

James broke the connection and made his way to the bathroom consumed is his anger. "So," he thought, "today I learnin' the truth."

God have mercy on the monster responsible for the gruesome rapes and murders, because that person would find no mercy in James!

A plan to handle the situation was developing in James' mind even as he joined Trish in the shower. An evil smile contorted James' angry features as his plan settled his resolve. He welcomed the chance to avenge Warren's death and also Dante's deception. Today would be a good day!

Chapter 5

"Stay in the car!" James growled, slamming the door.

Trish shivered in the stillness of his wake watching him storm toward the house. She saw him slide the pistol out from under his shirt and step lightly onto the porch of the weathered wood frame house. The un-kept grounds coupled with the faded cracking paint gave the place a ramshackle appearance. The sight of the gun hadn't really surprised her. James had become more sullen with the passing of every mile of their return trip. By the time they'd pulled to a stop moments ago, she could feel the fury he exuded. She had heard the lethal menace in his voice when he told her to *stay in the car*. She pitied whomever he had come here to see.

James crashed uninvited through the door, like a deadly, powerful hurricane wind. From his vantage point on the sofa Wes hadn't been able to see James drive up or approach the house. When the door crashed open he'd been caught completely off guard. Anger surged like fire through his veins, but the demon-like eyes glaring down the barrel of the revolver pointed at his face extinguished his blazing anger and froze his blood. The only heat that remained in his body burned in his lungs, reminding him that he hadn't drawn a breath since James busted in the door, yet he couldn't force himself to inhale. The furious, penetrating eyes staring at him commanded perfect stillness.

"I fuckin' want answers!" The ferocity in James' voice accented his words. "I am only asking the questions once. Understood?"

Unable to find his voice Wes nodded, confirming he understood completely.

"Who under cut my price?"

"Ja-Jason." Wes stuttered the name.

"Okay Wes, you're doing good." James paused gathering his thoughts. "Now this is real important Wes. Was the dope the same as the stuff I sold you?"

[33]

"Ye-Yeah."

"Are you sure?"

"Yeah." Wes, no longer under the gun, regained his confidence as James exited as swiftly as he had come.

~ ~ ~

Trish recognized David's house, as they slid to a bone jarring stop in the driveway.

David was coming off the porch as they stopped. He jogged to James' window and handed James a cordless phone. Shaking his head. "This is Wes." David indicated the caller. "He wants to talk to you."

James took the phone and pressed the off button then handed it back.

"What are you doing James?" David demanded, astonishment expressed in his tone and on his face.

"Going to see Dante." James stated through clenched teeth. "This is Trish; she's going to wait here with you until I get back." He pointed at Trish. "Out."

Trish didn't much care for being dropped off and for a moment she thought about protesting. Instead she leaned over and kissed James cheek. "Be careful," she whispered and got out of the car.

David, who had much a better idea of what was happening, was at a loss for words. All he could do was watch as James gunned the engine of the Corvette and raced away, tires screeching and smoking in his wake.

~ ~ ~

Encompassed in a 'Blood Rage' James, out of instinct more than conscious effort, sawed at the wheel, expertly bringing the cantering Corvette out of its fishtail, barely avoiding the white plank fence that crowded the asphalt drive. Exhaust roared from the tailpipes as the car lurched forward at near neck breaking speed and began gathering G-force like a Lear jet on a short runway. James could see the sprawling ranch house resting atop the knoll, growing ever larger as the powerful car shrunk the distance. At the last possible moment James whipped the car right, narrowly avoiding the marble maiden at her endless task of pouring water into the basin of the fountain that was at the center of the circular drive. A miracle feat of man and machine brought the car to an abrupt halt at the front walk.

James sprang from the car into the swirling dust and tire smoke, pistol in hand. Three occupants scattered out onto the veranda from the carved oak doors of the ominous dwelling. Two men, carrying shotguns with sawed-off barrels and pistol grips, framed the third man. The one James had come to see, Dante. Already on the walk James paused, gun pointed at Dante's chest, a lust for blood apparent in his icy blue-gray eyes.

"You fucked me Dante!" James snarled, growling his accusation. "Did you really think I wouldn't figure this out? It was all a lie wasn't it?" James continued his words, more statement than question. "You knew I wouldn't kill for no reason! So you come up with one hell of a reason! Warren wasn't the Rural Rapist was he? Why don't you tell me who took all those pictures of the crime scenes that you supposedly found in Warren's house?" James flicked the gun at the man to Dante's left. "What kind of psychopath are you Jason? The fact you get your kicks from raping and killing woman makes you a rabid dog. You need to be put down."

Dante stepped slightly forward spreading his arms, palms out, smirking. "Now James just calm down. Let's talk, you don't under~"

"I understand perfectly!" James cut him off. Thumbing the hammer back on his revolver as he spoke.

Dante surrendered the step he just taken, stepping back.

"You think people are your marionettes and you think you can just pull their strings so they will do your bidding. Well I ain't no fuckin' puppet. I killed a man based on your lies, now I'm going to kill you for those same lies and I'm going to kill that monster standing next to you." James again

[35]

indicated Jason with a flick of his gun. "I was wrong for killing Warren based on your lies and I have to live with that, but I can sure avenge his and Martha's death."

"Now James," Dante's voice low and condescending, his eyes flat, and emotionless. "Take a measure of the odds; you have two shotguns pointed at you. You can't win."

James shrugged, shaking his head, still snarling his hate and contempt, voice eerie and calm. "Dante I may not win here, but I'll take you to hell with me, count on that."

James saw the blur of movement too late. The blow sent a Milky Way of stars swirling and dancing before his eyes then he was consumed by darkness. Excruciating pain flip-flopped his stomach; a cloudy sky swam in and out of focus as he struggled to swallow the bile rising in his throat. His every heartbeat throbbed in his head, showering his body in searing pain. A booted foot stomped his shoulder and denied his clawing attempt to rise. Dante peered down at him, a sarcastic scowl on his face.

"Tsk tsk tsk, James." Dante taunted, shaking his head, his salt-and-pepper hair framing his sun-lined face. "Not a real smart move, son. Now listen carefully. I'm only going to say this once."

James lay motionless, glaring at the aging Dante.

"You get in that car, and drive away, and forget what you think you know." Dante stepped back and motioned to his henchmen. "You two, help James to his car."

The two roughly dragged James to his feet, shoving him toward the car.

"James," Dante called out. "Don't come back, you hear?"

James plopped into the driver's seat, blood cascading through his hair onto his shoulder. Sagging over the wheel, still not quite able to shake off the haze of the heavy blow to the head, James wordlessly retreated down the drive.

~ ~ ~

"James." Trish and David said collectively, as James stumbled through David's front door.

"What the fuck happened to you?" David asked, offering James help to the couch.

James pushed his friend and the offered help away. "I made a mistake. I underestimated Dante. It won't happen again."

"You need to go to the hospital," Trish said evaluating James' injuries at a distance.

"The hell I will," James sat heavily on the couch.

"We can handle this," David said taking control. "Trish take my car to the store and pick up some rubbing alcohol to clean the cut on James' head." David handed her the keys and a wad of cash. "And hurry up."

Trish took the keys and the cash, hustling out the door. The short drive to the corner store gave her time to think. She hadn't been away from James long enough in the past two weeks to check in and she knew Russo well enough to know he would be furious with her.

She parked in front of the store and rushed to the payphone, dialing the number she knew by heart.

"Russo." He answered on the fourth ring.

"It's me –"

"Where the fuck are you?" Russo shouted into the receiver.

"At a pay phone in Pinecrest" Trish's answer was just above a whisper

"I thought I told you to keep me posted on James' whereabouts."

"I haven't been able to call before now."

"Well try harder."

"I will."

"You better. Now where's James?" Russo asked.

"He's with his partner David and he's beat up pretty bad. Some guy named Dante beat him up."

"Have you heard of this Dante guy before?"

"No." Trish answered.

"Well if you hear his name again, listen closely and let me know immediately what is said. You got that?"

"I will."

"Now what else have you heard."

"Not much. James doesn't say much in my presence. I went with him to West Palm. He sold some drugs down there but I don't know to who."

"Alright."

When Russo hung up Trish couldn't have been happier. She hated him. If she could only find a way to escape him, she would. But she'd tried before and was rewarded with one helluva beating when he found her. An involuntary shiver passed through her at the memory.

She'd only been 16 when she met him. She was living on the streets, hooking to eat, a runaway with not a place to go. He'd taken her home and treated her kind, but not for long, soon he had her dancing in his club and turning tricks. How many years had passed since then? No matter, she didn't care to remember.

Chapter 6

THREE MONTHS LATER

"Mayhew, the Captain wants to see you in his office ASAP."

Mayhew hadn't noticed the Captain's secretary until she spoke. She was in her usual attire – skirt and a blouse, both at least two sizes too small – with her holier than thou aloofness dripping through her movements. He wondered, not for the first time, if the were rumors were true. Was the captain – a married man – screwing his 'sexretary', the name given to her by many of the officers behind her back.

"Close the door." The captain said, from behind his mahogany desk.

Mayhew took notice of the stranger seated in one of the arm-chairs in front of the desk. By the look of her she was a Fed – smart business suit, no makeup her auburn hair styled at shoulder length. He glanced back at the Captain, a burly overweight man, his stern pockmarked face always serious and intimidating. The kind of face that naturally scared small children.

"What's up Capt.?" Mayhem always called him 'Capt.' knowing full well it annoyed him.

"Sit down Mayhew."

He took the vacant chair next to the stranger giving her a slight nod in greeting.

"This is agent Brooks from the D.E.A.." In an amicable way, the Captain indicated the stranger with an outstretched hand. "It would appear," he continued, "that your current case overlaps an ongoing D.E.A. Investigation. Apparently Dante Westhardt is the subject of a methamphetamine manufacturing and distribution organization. Agent Brooks."

"Detective Mayhew." She began in a pinched, obviously Southern voice. "It's my understanding you are working the homicide cases of Martha Westhardt and Warren Allison?"

Mayhew facing her, nodded, signifying he was.

"We've been working undercover for more than a year trying to get evidence against Westhardt. So far all our efforts have been in vain, but this new turn of events has brought about an urgency to come up with something, anything to bring him in. The problem is we haven't been able to get anyone inside. It's a tight knitted group out there and I'm sure I don't have to tell you that it's a dangerous place for strangers."

Mayhew shot a questioning look at his Captain who in turn shrugged defensively as if to say *my hands are tied.* He turned back to Brooks knowing now she was going to pull rank on him.

"You see," she said in a nasal monotone, "I've been undercover on this thing for quite some time and we don't want you to do anything to compromise my position."

"And just what is your position?" Mayhew inquired.

"Have you ever heard of Jason Tess?"

"I met him in fact, a few weeks ago at Westhardt's ranch."

She gave him a knowing look.

"He showed me the guest house where Warren Allison lived."

"He failed to show up for a big party that same night. You see, we figure the only way to get a stranger inside is through deep cover."

The words stunned Mayhew. He couldn't help but wonder how far she'd gone or would go in the name of the investigation.

"What we want you to do is back off, Detective. The fact is, that if we're right in our thoughts concerning the murders, they will become part of a Federal indictment. Basically speaking this is our case." Brooks walked to the door. "I have work to do gentlemen. Thanks for your time." Hastily, with that she was gone.

Mayhew propped his elbows on his knee cradling his 5 o'clock shadow covered chin in his hands. He stared blankly at the clutter that blanketed the Captain's desk, not really noticing the organized disarray, but finding it or the situation mesmerizing.

"What the fuck was that?" Mayhew said, settling his harsh distant glare on the Captain. He sprang to his feet throwing his arms up in exasperation. "Don't answer that Capt." Scarcely controlling his anger he stormed from the Captain's office.

~ ~ ~

"Let's go Dave!" James shouted, as he finished packing the car

Trish – wearing a half shirt, cutoff jean shorts and sandals leaned, arms crossed, against the car and spoke. "You seem to be in a good mood today James."

"Why wouldn't I be?" He asked as he closed the hatchback. "I have a beautiful woman and my best friend with me. We're going to West Palm to sell a quarter million dollars' worth of crank. So what's not to be happy about?"

"I'm worried, James." She said seriously.

"What's wrong baby?" He put his hands on her hips as he spoke, to comfort her.

"It's really none of my business." She looked away from his cobalt gaze. "But," she stammered. "I really like, maybe love you, and I'm worried something bad is going to happen to you."

Her words caught him off guard.

"It's just that," she continued. "After you were beat-up a few weeks ago it reminded me how dangerous drugs can be. I know you're making a lot of money but when is enough - enough?"

"Look Trish," he pulled her close. "I got caught slipping, but everything worked out. Going to Dante's house in anger was a mistake, one that I won't make again."

"You two *Lovebirds* ready?" David teased.

[41]

"Yeah," James responded, glad for the interruption. "You're driving," he said tossing the keys to David.

"Are you sure you trust me to drive your car?"

"If you think I'm going to drive while my girl rides in your lap, you're crazy!" James chided as Trish climbed in on his lap.

"It was worth a try." David laughed, pulling onto the highway.

"Hey Dave, I've been thinking. We are piling up some cash. What do you think about buying some Gold Eagles?" James asked, two hours into the trip.

David glanced at his friend, arching one eyebrow. "Why Gold Eagles?"

"Well, we can't put the money in the bank. Gold Eagles will sure store better than cash. Besides, at some point we're gonna to have to save enough to get out of the dope game." James gently squeezed Trish's thigh where he'd been resting his hand.

"Why the sudden concern over getting out?" David questioned with another quick glance in James' direction.

"Just thinking of the future." James said offhandedly. "What have we made now? Seven, eight hundred thousand?"

"Yeah, about seven-fifty." David answered after some thought.

"What's it been, six months?" James asked.

"Yeah, about that. What're you thinking James?"

"Well... I'm thinking, we're making some pretty big waves if you get my meaning. And we started this whole thing with a big splash." James stated.

Trish listened intently, but said nothing. "This thing with Dante bothering you?" David inquired

"Maybe a little, but you know how Keysville is. It doesn't take long before everyone knows your business." James paused "And that bothers me."

"So what is it you want me to do James?"

[42]

"Take half my money and buy Gold Eagles with it." James answered then added "remember not to spend too much in one place we don't want to draw any attention to us."

"I'll handle it James." David said as he parked in front of the hotel.

James handed Trish a stack of hundreds. "Get us a two room suite baby." He kissed her. "We'll be back in a while. Call me and let me know the room number."

"Be careful James." Trish's voice cracked, betraying her nervousness.

James glimpsed the shimmer of tears in her eyes as she turned away. What was he going to do with her? He wasn't sure. He was fond of her, but it sure wasn't love for him. What had she said? *'Maybe Love'* he'd have to consider that. He watched her walk into the lobby of the hotel and it occurred to him that the front desk clerk was in for a thrill, her in a half shirt, bra-less and tight cutoffs. He smiled inwardly but he felt a tinge of jealousy. Might it be time to move on?

"Which way?" David questioned.

"Huh?"

"Which way?" David asked a second time.

"Oh. Left." James pointed.

"So, what are we going to do about Dante and Jason?" David asked, piloting the car into traffic.

"I know what I want to do." James said, fingering the still tender spot where he'd been struck on the head at the hands of one of Dante's henchmen.

"I still don't believe Jason is the Rural Rapist.

"You better," James stated. "Because he is, and furthermore he is a psycho piece of shit. He needs killing."

"Yeah, and it has to be him because he has the recipe. No other reason for Dante to give it to him." David speculated. "Yeah, he's a sicko."

"Remember his last victim, Dante stood there and watched." James shook his head in disgust. "I think we

[43]

should kill them." David let James' word hang between them for a few moments before he spoke. "I'm not disagreeing with you James, but maybe we should let things cool down a bit first. It's only been six months."

"Yeah. You're probably right." James' thoughts drifted back to the night he murdered Warren. He often thought about that night and it always left him hollow inside. He had killed an innocent man, because Dante had convinced him Warren was the Rural Rapist. Now he was forced to live with the bitter truth...

~ ~ ~

Paul's girlfriend answered the door and let James and David into the sprawling beach front house. The partners followed the petite woman to the back of the dwelling where their most recent customer shot pool in a game room.

"What's up," James said in greeting, tossing the canvas bag containing twenty pounds of meth on the pool table, sending balls scattering. "This is my partner David."

Paul nodded leaning on his pool cue.

"That's twenty in the bag," James tried to break the tension that was always a factor in the dope business when strangers met.

"Three hundred. Right?" Paul asked, gathering the balls and placing them in the rack.

"Yeah, and I talked to David about your offer. 10 apiece, but you've gotta take a hundred."

"That's a million a shot," Paul said after quickly figuring.

"But it's a helluva deal," David shot in return.

"I don't have that kinda cash fellas..."

"Well, what's that boat worth out there?" James asked pointing at the yacht tied to the dock.

"About half that." Paul answered. "Why? Are you looking for a boat?"

"I might be. You got the cash to cover the rest?"

"I will have after a couple more turn-overs."

"We'll deal then." James took one last glance at the yacht. "How 'bout the cash for this delivery?"

Paul walked over to the bar in the corner and reached for a bag. With a grunt he hefted the heavy bag and return.

"Do I need to count it?" James asked handing the bag to David.

"Come on, you know better."

James smiled. "See you next month..."

~ ~ ~

James answered his cell phone on the third ring. "Yeah."

"James?"

"Yeah."

Trish's voice sounded small and metallic in the receiver.

"What's up, baby?"

"I'm in suite 1420," Trish answered. "They gave me complimentary tickets to a comedy club, can we go?"

"Who gave you tickets?"

"The desk clerk when I checked in. Can we go?" Trish asked.

"When is the show?"

"Tonight at eight."

"If you want to go honey, we'll go." James said. "We're on our way back now. We should be there in a few minutes."

"Trish?" David asked the rhetorical question.

James nodded pushing the off button on his phone. "She wants to go to some comedy show in Coconut Grove."

"What's up with you and her James?"

James shook his head at the unexpected question. "Haven't really thought about it." James said. "Just kinda having fun. She's pretty – keeps me warm at night. What else can I say?"

David studied his friends face, quietly wondering if he should press the issue. Throwing caution to the wind he asked. "What if she leaves? I mean she knows too much."

"She won't." James said with confidence.

"She won't what?" David asked, "leave or talk?"

"Neither." James responded, still confident.

"I hope you're right." David let the statement hang.

~ ~ ~

"You were wrong Uncle Dante!" Wes' face contorted in contempt. "You should have never lied to James."

"Whose side you on boy?" Dante' words rang through the house like a shot from a rifle.

"I'm not taking a side on this one." Wes sprang to his feet and began pacing the length of the den.

"It would seem to me *'No Choice'* is taking sides against me."

"Boy when your parents died I raised you like a son and now you'd betray me?"

Wes spun to face Dante barely able to contain his own anger; his voice trembled when at last he spoke. "You betrayed yourself. James would have never killed Warren had he known the truth, but you tricked him. Now it appears you've outsmarted yourself. I wouldn't want to be in your shoes, because James will get even! Ask Jason; God only knows he and James have had their share of run-ins."

Jason had watched the argument wordlessly from the corner of the room. At the mention of his name he shifted uncomfortably in his chair.

"What's your take on this?" Dante demanded, his icy glare falling on Jason like a chilly shadow.

"Wes is right about James." Jason mumbled. At that moment Jason hated Wes for dragging him into the argument. He didn't like being on the *'Hot Seat'* and by the look in Dante's eyes that was precisely where he was at.

"So you too, think James will come after me?" Dante fired back.

"I think he will." Jason answered.

Wes was shaking his head in an *'I told you so'* nod.

"Can you take him out?" Dante asked Jason.

"Are you crazy?" Wes shouted in disbelief. "We already have a homicide detective asking questions and now you want to kill someone else. You've lost your mind."

Jason was momentarily relieved, as Dantes' head snapped around in Wes' direction, but the unexpected turn of events, he knew, was cause for concern. He of all people knew how dangerous James, with his uncanny luck could be. Lost in his dilemma he blankly stared at the intricately carved red oak coffee table.

"You've become an old fool," Wes growled through gritted teeth. "And I want nothing to do with this, or you." Wes stormed up the steps toward the door.

"If you leave boy, don't ever come back."

"You can bet I won't," came Wes' response never missing a step, his boot heels echoing off the marble foyer floor.

"Can you?" Dante shouted, turning back to Jason.

It took Jason a moment to realize the words were directed at him. "What?" He stammered.

"Can you kill James?" Dante's words were more demand than question.

"Yeah. I think I can..."

"Don't think boy!" Dante roared. "Can you or can't you?"

Jason trembled. "I'll do it." His voice weak and unsteady.

"That's my boy." Dante said patting Jason's shoulder like he was a grade schooler. "Now, I want it done a little differently this time. I do not want his body found. Bury him in the swamps. You hear?"

"Whatever you want."

"Good. Then we'll bury that traitor nephew of mine right next to him." Dante's words hung in the air like dense, early morning fog.

Chapter 7

The three ambled up the cobblestone street of Coco Walk. The early evening crowd moved in various size groups, seeming to have no more in common than their thin pastel colored clothing worn defensively against the stifling Florida heat. The South Florida elite had long ago, custom tailored, Coconut Grove to suit their flaunting ways. Quaint as it appeared on the surface with its personalized shops and laid-back atmosphere, wealth was the pinnacle of society here. The working class were paid well for the tasks they performed, but the lifeblood of the community was the powerfully wealthy.

They threaded their way through the animated throngs, gathering in the festiveness, ascended a flight of stairs and found a table along the terrace rail overlooking the busy cobblestone walk. Trish excused herself to search out the ladies room as James and David took their seats. Both men watched her move along the crowded terrace, her platinum blonde hair cascading over her graceful slender shoulders, her slim waist giving way to ample hips, her short skirt revealing long shapely legs the impossible rake of her spiked heels accenting the well-toned muscles of a dancer.

"I'll give you this." David stated matter-of-factly, "she is a beauty. You sure know how to pick'em."

James smiled a toothy smile at his friends' blunt admiration. "You too could possibly have a beauty like her, if you'd come out of your shell." He said tauntingly playful. "I'm serious."

What James intended to say David would never know. Something behind David caught James' attention that stopped him in mid-sentence. David turned to see what had enraptured his friend to the point of complete silence and in an instant, drained all color from James's face. David systematically scanned the open plaza not sure what he was searching for but sure he'd know it when he saw it. No commotion was apparent so he began to scan the faces, the ones closest first, working left to right. His eyes jumped from table to table until they descended on the polished hardwood bar. He eyed the patrons occupying the stationary stools that framed the curved edge of the hardwood bar. Movement from behind the bar caught his attention. He turned toward the movement and like an angel she appeared. She had changed her hair color – she wore it short and blonde now, and had taken on the shape of a woman in the years since David had last seen her, forever leaving behind the look of the teenage girl she'd been the last time he had seen her, but there was no mistaking who she was. Her name flashed through David's mind. A name, in his mind, that would forever be synonymous with James. At the thought of his friend, he snapped around to again face him.

James, face slack, devoid of color, sat trancelike staring at her. Silently he mouthed her name *'Yvette'.* The flood of long forgotten emotions hit him like a sledgehammer casting the world around him into dense fog. Visibility was zero with one exception; he could see her with crystal clarity. He ran, first finding the stairs, he descended through the fog spilling out onto the cobblestone street in a blind, stumbling jog. Absentmindedly he bumped into other pedestrians causing a commotion in his wake, but oblivious to anything except the turmoil inside. He was breathless when he reached his car, his every gulp for air overruled by the constriction in his chest. Seconds later he raced blindly into the blackness of the night.

From the open terrace rail, David watched the spectacle of James' retreat. He had called out to him, but to no avail. He could only imagine at what James was going through. The endless flood of memories that must be streaming through his mind.

"David."

Trish's voice tore him from his thoughts, instinctively he spun to face her.

"Where's James?" She asked.

[50]

"Um, well... ah... 'He had to go take care of something." He stumbled through the lie. Unprepared for the question, but recovering quickly he continued. "James asked me to take you back to the hotel and wait for him."

"But what about the show?" She protested, folding her arms under her breasts in anger.

"I'm sure James will make it up to you." He said, leading her by the arm toward the parking lot.

"What's going on, David?" She asked, as they walked.

"James got an urgent call." He lied again.

"It's not trouble is it?" Concern laced her voice.

Trouble, he thought, *you have no idea!* "No, just business," he said wishing it were true. But, he knew James would handle it. James always handled it, no matter what it was. James just had an uncanny knack for prevailing. Although David knew things were about to become real interesting.

Miles away James found himself stopped at a green light. The car behind him encouraging him on with a persistent horn blast. He made a right-hand turn, then another into a deserted parking lot of an auto repair shop, the mechanics long since gone for the day. There, in the parking lot he began to gather his ambushed thoughts. How could he have prepared for this? After all these years. He had thought of her often at first, but less as the years passed, and it had been months maybe a year since thoughts of her had invaded his mind. He had put her in the past, it had taken years, but time had pushed her out of memories reach at least until now. Now what? The reason of his mind tangled with emotion at the sight of her. Is she married? He hadn't thought to look for a wedding ring. Surely she'd found another.

James took out his syringe and mixed a powerful shot of methamphetamine and quickly injected it. Almost immediately he found solace in his drug altered state.

"Yeah." James answered the phone in the middle of its third ring.

"James?"

"What's up Dave?" James voice was thick and clipped under the influence of the drug.

"You okay?"

"Yeah." James' answer none too convincingly.

"Where are you at?"

"Tell the truth, I don't know. Some auto repair shop in West Palm." James looked around seeing his surroundings for the first time.

"Something wrong with the car?" David asked concerned.

"No, no, just stopped to collect my thoughts is all."

"Look, Trish and I are at the hotel. I told her you got an urgent call and had to go take care of something." David explained.

"Good man, sorry about leaving you. I don't know what came over me," James said with all sincerity.

"Don't worry about it, we're cool. When you coming back?"

"I don't know, I have to go see her Dave. Cover for me."

"Alright James."

James drove back to Cocoa Walk rehearsing in his mind what he would say. What's up? It's been awhile? How's it going? The memories surged back to the forefront of his mind. Their sweetness surged through him, enraptured him, took him back to youthful innocence. Slowly he relived them from the beginning to the end. *'THE END,'* the end tainted with the bitter-sweet memories. He parked where he could see the cobblestone walk from start to finish. His next thought was that of betrayal, her betrayal. She promised, but somehow she failed to keep that promise. A voice in his mind begged, pleaded: *'leave James, forget her, she's poison!'* He started the car, ready to heed the warning, but the gods of fate refused to be denied.

She strolled onto the cobblestones, her every step radiating confidence. Her cropped white-blond hair, rippling in the slight evening breeze, framing her stunning face. Emerald green eyes reflecting the artificial light along the walk. Delicately high cheekbones accented her aristcratly slim nose that gave way to sculpted full and perpetually moist lips. A sharp jaw line and narrow chin swept down to her sensual neckline and proud shoulders. Her breasts, full and firm, stretched a company logo printed on her T-shirt. She wore the shirt tied at the waist to accent her figure. Her cotton shorts were small and tight over generous hips that swayed with each graceful stride of her long, slender, smoothly tanned legs.

He pulled the car to the end of the stone walk blocking her approach. He tugged the tie from his long blonde hair absentmindedly and raked his fingers through his hair. Pushing the door open he climbed out before he lost his nerve. Resting his arms on the chest high roof of the Corvette he studied her as she walked toward him, not yet noticing him. He waited patiently knowing that the element of surprise had shifted to his side. He watched her carefree eyes dart to and fro taking in the familiar surroundings.

Her eyes first found the sleek midnight black Corvette, gliding over the polished, curved fenders, up the windshield and across the car's roof line, then her green eyes found his cobalt blue ones, stopping her dead in her tracks as if he were a ghost. Reflexively she brought a hand to her mouth and bit nervously on her first finger just above a perfectly sculpted salon nail. Recognition registered instantly on her face as tears glistened in her eyes. "James?" She said his name, almost to herself, in shocked disbelief.

He didn't respond, he couldn't trust his voice. Instead he contented himself to watch her reaction. The tears pooled in her eyes and spilled down her cheeks, leaving wet streaks in her makeup and still he said nothing.

As he strode around the back of the car, she took notice of the changes the years had made in him. His hair was much longer, flowing nearly to his waist. His eyes were ice, penetrating through her. His face hard, but handsome and more manly than she remembered. His silk shirt did little to hide his broad shoulders or flat stomach. His hips were narrow, and his stride was powerful and confident.

He opened the passenger door in wordless invitation.

Reluctantly she took painfully tiny steps, trapped in his encompassing icy gaze. She wanted to run. Find a safe haven from the piercing glaze that was melting her heart, but also spreading a chill through her. She shuddered involuntarily as he closed the door behind her en-capsuling her in his realm. How was this possible? How had he found her? Was he looking for her? Where was the shy boy she remembered? He was different now – she sensed it – harder somehow, bordering on evil. Where was he taking her? He hadn't spoken a word. Everything seemed surreal and he was driving like a man possessed with a death-wish. They were headed north along the coast, the outside world flashing by at a nauseating pace. She dared a glance at him; he stared straight ahead – his knuckles white from his death grip on the steering wheel. The overhead streetlights cast eerie shadows on the ghostly profile of his hollow appearing face. Miles outside of town, where the city gave way to the alabaster sand dunes of the coast, and parking lots, that by day were crowded with Yankees, boiled lobster red by the South Florida sun, he reached over and protectively placed his hand firmly on her chest above her breast and simultaneously jammed the brakes. She didn't have time to be startled by his touch because in an instant the car lurched sideways and catapulted into an empty parking lot. Her heart rate doubled and her fear for the moment held her anger at bay. Almost before the car stopped and long before she recovered her composure he was out of the car, his long strides effortlessly carrying him across the soft moonlit sands to the water's edge where the gentle Atlantic surf lapped at the beach and reflected a shimmering full moon. He heard the car door close, he knew she was coming. He could feel her presence as she drew closer. Why had he come back for her? His mind reeled for answers. She had, long ago, betrayed him and their love. He thought back to early May and his evil deed on a desolate country road. Dante had also betrayed him. In a much different situation, but the end result was the same. Both had left him to deal with the demons of loss. The chaos of his emotions were overwhelming him in pain and seething him in anger.

"I'm sorry James." Yvette's voice was small, barely audible above the surf. She couldn't see his expression when he turned to face her, but she could feel the fury of his glare. A sliver of moonlight moved over his features as he raked his hand through his long hair, his demonic look trapped the air in her lungs.

"Sorry!" He shouted, somewhere between disbelief and furious exasperation. "You betrayed me, our love, and now you're sorry? I have to admit, that's pretty original Yvette."

"What do you want from me?" She screamed defiantly. "We were young. Things change. So tell me what you want me to say?"

"Just tell me why you betrayed me?" He answered, with an inordinate calm, his voice insidiously smooth in its question, his ice cold blue eyes glittering in the moonlit darkness.

She folded her arms against the chill, that was more than the cool of the soft Atlantic breeze. "James," she stammered. "We were worlds apart, it just wouldn't have worked. It was better to let it go."

"Was it? Just like that, huh? Walk away?"

"James that's not fair."

"Fair! Mother fuckin' fair! What do you know about fair!" His voice dripped with disdain. "Can you even comprehend what I went through? What I'm still going through? You broke my heart you know. I can't even have a meaningful relationship with a woman because I refuse to put my heart on the line and I have you to thank."

"So you looked me up just to berate me?"

"I didn't look you up; I'm down here on business." He growled venomously.

"Nice car, business must be good." She said trying to change the direction of their conversation desperately.

"I doubt you'd approve, but I am my father's son, and besides it pays the bills."

She closed the distance between them if only physically. "You're down here alone?" She asked not more than an inch of salt laced air between them.

"No." He said flatly.

"Who's with you?" She questioned catching a lock of his silky hair with her graceful fingers, stroking it.

"Dave and Trish."

She arched a questioning eyebrow at Trish's name.

"I've been seeing her for a few months or so." He elaborated. "She's a stripper."

"Serious?"

"I haven't really considered it that much."

"Where's she now?"

"At the hotel with Dave."

"She know you're with me?"

He shook his head placing his trembling hands on her hips. "I've missed you." He said brushing a kiss across her lips, then quickly broke their embrace.

She watched him turn warily to face the white crested, untamed waves breaking in a tumbling surge on the beach sands. He was different how – time had changed him – he'd grown into a man, but the change was far more than that. And his eyes, once a sanctuary of inspiration, now seemed more a malicious domain of barbaric evil, ready to devour her. Yet she could still feel the faint kiss he'd hastily graced across her lips, igniting an infectious, lethal fire with his spark. She should flee this place; too much time had gone by. She should just turn and walk away, but he intrigued her sinfully. She wrapped her arms around his waist laying her face against his flowing blonde hair taking in his once familiar scent. He wasn't a large man, but where

[56]

her hands lay on his abdomen she could feel the ripples of hard flesh, and his broad back had the unmistakable mounds of bunched muscle. For the first time she wondered at what his life had been like since they'd last been together. What had put that sinister elusiveness in his once brilliant eyes? How could he have changed so drastically in a short period of time? Was she to blame? Had she turned his heart, a heart that once was an open book, so cold?

The quickness of his agile movement startled her; fluidly he rotated in her embrace, one of his powerful hands finding the small of her back forcing her against him. The other equally powerful hand - full of her hair turned her face up to meet the crushing blow of his lips on hers. His demanding tongue explored her mouth with a violent need. If she had had any doubts about his strength they were now dispelled. His embrace was ironclad and hot as molten steel, but his urgency frightened her. Precariously she hung in the balance between pandemonium of her fear and the temptation of his wicked salvation. Her world, a world she had always ruled omni-potently, was crumbling to his unyielding demand for her surrender. He was invading the sanctuary of the carefully laid walls around her heart. Not to stop him, she knew was dangerous, but her defenses had fled in the face of his intrusiveness. She struggled to regain control to any degree, but control eluded her, all caution thrown to the wind. She could blame no one but herself. She'd compromised herself when she'd embraced him. Now she was tangled in the web he was weaving around her.

For months after she'd left, every night had been torture for him. He clearly remembered fighting off sleep, knowing she'd come in his dreams, and in the morning he'd wake alone. For years he'd thought of her, tormenting himself. Then he'd taught himself to hate her in defense of his sanity, but here, in her arms, his hate faded. He wanted, no, needed her. He pulled her tight T-shirt off, throwing it to the sand. She was bra-less, her breasts firm and pert, nipples erect, were perfectly visible in the moon's light. She stepped back leaving her slide-on sandals where she'd stood. Without a second thought she wiggled out of her cotton shorts and panties. She was still the most brash and beautiful woman he'd ever known.

"We've played this game before, haven't we James?" She said smiling wickedly, confident in her nakedness.

He was so transfixed by her beauty that he barely heard her words. She'd done it again − challenged him − after all these years. Well, he had stood his ground then and he would now. He kicked off his boots, then never breaking eye contact with her, he removed his own clothing. He extended a hand to her, she accepted, and he led her into the cool Atlantic water. They waded past the point where the swells broke into white crested waves. Again he pulled her close in the ever-changing water depth, her delicately soft body in complete contrast to his steely hardness. He kissed her.

Timing the water perfectly she rode a chest-deep swell until she was able to wrap her legs around his waist and with a familiarity that transcended the years, she rode the receding swell down onto his manhood. A sharp intake of her breath as he entered her was followed by a moan as he cradled her buttocks in his powerful grip, expertly guiding her over him to the lazy natural rhythm of the swells. Both were content to let nature dictate the pace, to take a natural crescendo to physical bliss.

In the waning darkness of predawn, back in the car, they sat in silence watching purples push the blackness of night off the eastern horizon only to be forced away by pinks and blues.

James' cell phone disturb the relaxed stillness of morning. He glanced at Yvette, her magnificent face still flushed from their foray in the Atlantic. She stared back at him, imploring him with her eyes not to answer the phone, not to break the magic of the moment.

"Yeah." He answered on the fifth ring.

Yvette frowned her disapproval.

[58]

"James?" Where've you been? I been trying to reach you all night." The voice on the line was frantic.

"Wes?" James said confused. "What's up?"

"We have to talk." Wes' words were clipped, demanding. "It's a matter of life and death, your life or death."

"What the fuck you talking about?" James' anger rose quickly in his voice. He watched Yvette's expression change from dismay to concern.

"Let's not do this on the phone James. Can you meet me somewhere?"

"I'm not in Keysville right now, but I can be there tonight. Say 9 o'clock at Lillie Bridge. And Wes, this had better be good."

"I'll be there, friendly piece of advice James, be real careful until we talk." Wes said and the line went dead.

James laid the phone down and started the car, shaking his head as he pulled away.

"What was that all about?" Yvette asked.

"Something's come up, I have to get back to Keysville."

"Everything alight?"

"Yeah. Just business," he responded.

"And what business might that be?"

"Not now Yvette. Please."

"So that's it, huh? You're gonna drop me off, wham-bam-thank-you-ma'am?" She asked, not trying to conceal her bitterness.

"God dammit Yvette! Don't start. It's not like that, but something real important has come up," he shot back just as bitter.

"Oh. More important than me?" She accused.

"Give me a break here." He pleaded angrily. "A lot is going on you know nothing about. People's lives could be at stake, maybe mine."

She didn't respond.

They rode in silence that would match that of the trip they'd made in the other direction hours earlier. He stopped at the only car in the Cocoa Walk parking lot, rightfully assuming it was hers.

"I'm sorry, James. About everything." She said sincerely. "Will I see you again?"

"I'll be down here this time next week." He answered avoiding the direct question, and her tear filled emerald eyes.

"I work nights, Thursday to Sunday." She stated flatly. "I still love you James."

He watched her walk to the small four-door sedan and drive away.

Chapter 8

James entered the hotel suite quietly. The only light was coming from a wall fixture above the complimentary liquor cabinet. He emptied two of the small bottles into a tumbler, not even caring to check what names were on their labels. He gave the tumbler a quick swirl and emptied it in two gulps cringing at the taste of the combination of brandy and scotch, but the warmth spreading through his chest and in his stomach was giving him the desired effect. He heard a door swing slowly open and he knew without looking who it was.

"James."

It was the voice he'd expected.

"Are you alright?" Trish asked.

Boy, he thought, is that a loaded question. I'm just fine. I left you in a bar last night for David to take care of. Then spent the night on the beach with a long-lost love. Only to get a life or death phone call this morning. "I'm fine," is all he said.

She wrapped her arms around his waist from behind. "Oh. Your hairs wet, and you smell like you've been at the beach?"

"It's a long story," he responded to her implied question. "We'll talk about it later," he said, closing the subject before this got out of hand. God what a mess, he thought. What else could possibly go wrong to more complicate his life. This was supposed to be easy street, nothing but a good time. So far it's been a hell of a hassle.

"James."

"Yeah baby."

"Can I tell you something?"

"Sure."

"I'm pregnant."

'Oh shit'! The words were so loud in his mind for a moment he wasn't sure that he hadn't screamed them out loud. Well James, you had to ask, he thought, and then his

face paled as he thought of the James family curse. "Are you sure?" He asked, his voice low and trembley. Neither his grandfather, nor his father had seen their child born and both were killed by police in gun battles. The end was near; the curse lived.

"Are you happy James?" She whispered, tensely awaiting his response.

"I'm happy baby," he lied. But he didn't think she could handle what he believed to be the truth about his impending fate. "I need a shower, baby," he said, breaking her embrace. "Get your things together, we have to get back to Keysville. Something's come up." He started toward the bathroom door.

"James."

He half turned to face her.

"I'm just late, but I'm pretty sure."

He walked to the bathroom without responding...

~ ~ ~

The brownish-green sawgrass rushed past the window as David navigated the Corvette down the two lane highway known as Alligator Alley. The silence in the car was loud and heavy with thought. Trish, from her vantage point on James' lap, her back against the passenger door, was content to stare at the basic nothingness of the repetitious sawgrass covering the swampy planes.

"So, what's going on James, that it's so important we leave at eight in the morning hell-bent on gettin' back to Keysville?" David's voice seemed to boom in the silence.

"Not now, Dave," James said evenly.

Trish shifted uncomfortably on James' lap, understanding the discussion was not meant for her ears, but she said nothing. James had been in a foul mood all morning and she had no desire to agitate him. She just hoped that 'business' as he called it was the cause for his mood and not her decision to announce she was pregnant. She was expected to keep tabs on him and although she had

had a change of heart she wasn't sure changing sides was an option. "Dave," he said. "I need you to take care of a few things for me if you will?"

"Name it, James."

"I want you to take Trish to get a hotel room in Bradon." He squeezed her knee affectionately as he spoke. "Then take her to get anything she needs – anything. I don't care what it costs."

David glanced first at Trish then to James. "What are you going to do?"

"Take care of the situation. And until I do, I don't want Trish anywhere near Keysville. I'm not sure what the hell is going on, but 'till I find out, I want to know she's safe."

Dave nodded his understanding.

Trish thought about protesting, but at James expression she thought better of it.

Chapter 9

James slowed the 900cc Ninja to make the precarious left-hand turn off the highway onto Jameson Road. It was more of a cowpath than a road, the uneven surface was made up of tar and pea gravel and snaked its way through pastureland and long forgotten pits that had been dug to strip the phosphate and sulfur from the mineral rich soil. He navigated the powerful motorcycle at deadly speed, with the precision and confidence that comes from years of traveling the same route. He was early for the rural meeting, but years in the drug trade had taught him caution.

Slowly as he crossed Lillie Bridge he scanned the ancient live oaks and palmetto bushes for movement. The desolate bridge was perfect for a private discussion, but too, it was perfect for an ambush. Satisfied it was safe, he turned around and rode back onto the narrow concrete bridge and shut off the motorcycle. He pulled off his helmet and walked over and sat down on the galvanized guardrail to wait.

The light of day was rapidly receding, making way for the darkness of night. The weight of the events that had unfolded in the past twenty-four hours lay heavily on his mind. He fished a cigarette from his pocket and lit it. When he exhaled, the blue-gray smoke swirled in the waning light. The crickets stroked their legs together sending their fiddle like mating call out to all in earshot, a sure sign of the encroachment of night. The river water trickled beneath the bridge ever so slightly giving a peaceful tranquility to the secluded place. However, none of these surroundings could still the turmoil James felt inside. Seeing Yvette again after all these years had caught him off guard, like a right hook from the blindside. Before he even had a chance to recover from the blow, Trish had struck him with her news of pregnancy. He was sure that the news Wes had for him was no revelation that would solve all his problems. At the thought of Wes he absentmindedly touched the hardwood grip on the .357 tucked in his black leather riding jacket. His gloved fingers glided smoothly over the pistol comforting him.

In the silence, the weight of the past six months seemed to descend on him like an unbearable load. James knew all his recent actions had been reaction, and too, he knew, that if he intended to succeed he must stop reacting and take the offensive. With that thought fresh in his mind, he began to formulate a plan of action in his mind. His plan was a flexible, and evolving, but also a plan of advancement and action.

The driving sound of a high-performance engine brought him out of the reverie of his plotting. James crushed out the stub of his cigarette and stood waiting, attempting, in vain, to calm his nerves.

He studied the monstrous four-wheel-drive truck as it approached; searching for the slightest indication that something was amiss. When Wes jumped down from the driver's seat, James' shoulder and back muscles involuntary hunched, as his senses went on 'high alert'.

"What's up, James?" Wes asked, as he approached him, offering his hand.

"You tell me," James warily gave Wes' hand a firm shake.

"I don't know how to say this, so I'll just give it to you straight. Dante ordered Jason to kill you."

James began to pace contemplating Wes' revelation.

"I know what you're thinking," Wes said, cautiously.

James stopped in front of Wes glaring at him, "Do ya?"

Wes nodded, accepting the actions his words would bring about.

"Where do you stand Wes?"

"Out in the cold." The answer came quick with a ring of truth.

James began to pace again. "I'll tell you Wes, I owe you one. So here's the deal, take it or leave it. We go together and take out Jason, tonight. I won't ask you to go when I take Dante down, him being your uncle and all, but we do Jason together, in for a penny in for a pound. I'll cut you in on my business − five percent − that's about 10 maybe 20,000 a month. It's up to you?"

"Would you let me walk away, knowing how much I know?"

"I don't know," James said knowing damn well he wouldn't; he couldn't take the chance. "And Dante won't, even if I would," he added.

Wes was nobody's fool. He knew the rules of contraband well. They all did; they'd been doing this for years. The stakes had changed at every level; from street-level dealers, to the wholesalers, to manufacturers. He'd started to worry, at the street-level, like James, he'd been unwilling to kill to achieve the coveted highest rank. But the rules remained the same. James couldn't let him walk and neither could Dante. Wes knew it. They had all agreed to play by these rules long ago. The law of this jungle, that had become their lives, was that a man must keep his secrets, and cover his tracks at all costs. "I'm in," Wes said at last.

"You sure Wes? There ain't no road back from where we're headed."

"I'm sure, let's just get this over with."

"I like your spirit Wes, that's my sentiments exactly." James smiled to hide his own distaste for the situation. "This is what we do; we'll park in the orange grove about a quarter-mile from his house. Then we'll walk through the grove, around behind the house, and I'll go in the back door, while you cover the front, from the corner of the house. Once we get him, we'll take him out back. He ain't got no close neighbors, so no one should hear the shot. We'll shoot him in the head, so he won't bleed much, plus we'll be able to wrap his head in a trash bag so we don't get blood in the bed of your truck. Once we have him in the truck, you can drive out to Hopewell Road in the truck. I'm gonna use the hose and wash down any blood on the grass. Then I'll meet you on Hopewell Road. We'll take him out to the back pit.

There's some sand flats out there where we can bury him. Got it?"

"Yeah."

"Good. Oh, hey Wes."

"Yeah."

"Don't let me forget to grab a shovel while we're at Jason's."

~ ~ ~

The miles seem to be passing quicker than the speed Wes was driving would allow. Maybe, he thought, it was because of his dread of what lay ahead. He was scared, more afraid than he'd ever been in his life, but he knew that he couldn't let his fear show. At this point a show of fear could be the death of him. He kept reminding himself what Jason had done to those women. It was a futile attempt to convince himself that Jason had this coming – deserved it even. A quick glance at the headlight of James' motorcycle in his rearview mirror reminded him of another reason why Jason had this coming. James had no choice but to strike first, his life depended on it. Still, Wes found no solace in his resolve that they were doing the right thing.

West turned off the road onto one of the sugar sand lanes, that separated the narrow straight rows of manicured, 20 foot tall orange trees. When he climbed from the truck the night air was hot, and sticky, and heavy with moisture, making it hard to draw his next breath. He tried to ignore the feeling of breathlessness, he'd lived his whole life in Central Florida, and the stifling heat was certainly nothing new. He reached under his seat, slipping his .38 Special Smith & Wesson out from its case. The gun, ironically enough, had been a gift from his uncle Dante. How fitting he intended to use it to murder his uncle's illegitimate son.

"You ready?"

James' voice startled him. "Yeah." He answered truthfully. He was ready – ready to get this over with and get the hell out of this place.

"Follow me." James ordered. The pair started off, passing between the thorn covered branches of row after row of orange trees. Carefully stepping over the aboveground sprinkler pipes, the soft sand caved in under their weight, making each step difficult and strained. By the time they reached the edge of Jason's yard, both were breathing hard and sweating profusely. They knelt together under a tree, where they had an unobscured view of the backyard.

"Thirty-seven." James whispered.

"Thirty-seven what?"

"Thirty-seven rows of trees between here and where we parked." James answered. "Now let's go."

They were halfway across the yard when they heard a woman scream for help, followed by the unmistakable sound of an openhanded slap on flesh. They covered the remaining ground to the back door quickly.

The house was an old wood-frame with a tin roof that did little to muffle the commotion inside with its clapboard walls. They could hear the whimpering pleas of a woman begging not to be hurt. The cries for mercy were met by hysterically evil laughter and then a voice both men knew well. "Quit fighting it bitch. You 'n' me gonna have some fun one way or another." The voice was followed by another slap.

James had heard enough, he drew his revolver with his right hand, trying the door with the other. The knob turned at his urging. He opened the door slightly, far enough to peer inside. He could see the mismatched washer and dryer to the left just inside the door. There was a plaid couch thirty maybe forty feet away, in what appeared to be the front room, but the voice seemed to be coming from a hallway half the distance to the couch on the right. He swung the door open slowly, the old hinges creaking in protest, further alarming his pounding heart. With a sideways jerk of his head, he signaled Wes to follow him.

The pungent odor of spoiled trash greeted them as they entered the small laundry room. The well-worn and scarred hardwood slats that made up the flooring groaned under their weight, as they tiptoed along the cheaply paneled walls. At the entrance of the hallway they could hear Jason's threats clearly – 'I'll cut your fuckin' throat bitch'– coming from behind a door at the far end. They moved quickly down the hall careful not to make a sound. James tried the doorknob. "Locked" he mouthed silently to Wes. James squared his shoulders to the door, gripping his .357 Magnum in both hands, elbows bent at ninety degrees, barrel pointed at the ceiling, he thumbed the hammer of the revolver back until it locked. He raised his right leg and with all the force he could muster he stomped the flimsy door, barely missing the handle. The door crashed open, its jam splintering under the impact. In a fraction of a second James's mind registered the scene: a rickety old chest of drawers stood along the right paneled wall, a huge bed stripped of all linen took up most of the floor, the mattress stained and cocked on the spring box. Jason, bare from the waist up, skin covered in a thin sheen of sweat, face contorted insanely, psychopathic madness dancing dangerously in his eyes, held a hunting knife to the throat of an auburn haired woman. The woman – Jason holding her around the waist with this knife-less hand – wore nothing but a pair of panties. Blood ran freely from her nose, dripping from her chin to her bare chest. Her right cheek showing the purplish-blue of a fresh bruise.

"Drop the knife Jason!" James shouted leveling the gun at Jason's head.

Jason, recovering rapidly from the surprise of the intruders' sudden entrance, smiled wickedly. "James, I been looking for you."

"Drop the fuckin' knife asshole."

"What you gonna do James? Shoot me?" Jason laughed insanely, still caught in the web of madness. "I'm gonna kill her James. You can watch it if you wanta see how

[69]

a true killer works. 'Course I don't think you got the stomach for it." He taunted, pointing his knife at James. A mistake.

James' bullet entered Jason's brain through his right eye. The impact sent him crashing backwards through the room's only window, where his upper torso hung hideously halfway through the shattered pane of glass. The knife lay harmlessly on the floor below his dangling dead hand. Through the acrid smelling cloud of grayish gun-smoke James walked to the trembling woman, her face covered with her hands. Her shoulders slumped, jerking to the shudders of her sobs. He picked the beds coverlet off the floor and draped it around the woman's shoulders to cover her nakedness. One arm around her shaking shoulders he guided her from the room. "Find a washcloth and something for her to wear." He barked at Wes.

In the dimly lit living room he sat her down on the plaid couch. The amber light was supplied by a corner lamp, its shade nicotine stained and dingy. Wes handed James a damp cloth and tossed a few articles of clothing on the sofa. "Go drag that piece of shit out the window and check outside to make sure everything's cool," James ordered. He turned his attention back to the woman who was obviously in shock. Gently he pulled her bloodstained hands away from her battered face. Softly whispering, reassuring words to her, he tenderly began to wipe away the blood on her face, chest, and hands. Her eyes were glazed over and showed no sign of comprehension of the world outside. Her tears continued to fall silently.

James pushed the coverlet back and helped her into the T-shirt Wes had brought, the shirt was far too large for her slight frame, as were the cut-off sweatpants, but James deftly tied the drawstring snugly at her slender waist. On a shelf in the corner sat a nearly full bottle of Jim Beam and a reasonably clean tumbler. He poured three fingers of the strong dark whiskey in the glass, and held it to her lips. She struggled to swallow, the amber liquid spilled from the corners of her trembling lips. Regaining a smidgen of her composure she accepted the glass from him, cradling it with her hands taking tiny sips. The warming effects of the whiskey, coupled with the mind-numbing power of alcohol urged her back to reality from her fugue state. Her first conscious sight, not shrouded in the pandemonium of fear, was him staring out the front window at the darkness. Who was this would-be savior of hers? So willing to kill for a total stranger? Where had he come from? Why was he here? He certainly hadn't been expected. She saw the slight tremble of his hand as he raised the squarish Jim Beam bottle to his lips and took a long hard pull. Her heart went out to him, whoever he was. He had saved her from certain rape and most likely death. She wondered if he would have been so quick to save her life if he knew who she really was, or more precisely what she was. "Thank you." She croaked out the words in a near inaudible whisper.

He turned sharply at the sound of her voice. *'Good*, he thought, *'she's coming out of it.'* He knew he needed to get this mess cleaned up, and get out of this place.

He had played the part of her "guardian angel", but his eyes belonged to no angel. They were cold, pale blue, alive with menace, that she somehow knew was not meant for her. Also, she saw the pain of inner suffering in an undercurrent of strength that far exceeded the physical realm.

"You okay ma'am?" His voice sounded resolute and commanding, even just above a whisper.

"I am now, thanks to you."

He waved away her words of gratitude modestly, and sloshed more whiskey in her glass. "Drink up!" He said. "This stuff won't cure ya, but it does wonders for the nerves." He smiled. "Where you from ma'am?"

"Tampa," she answered. "And you're making me feel old calling me ma'am. My name's Hope."

"Where 'bouts in Tampa?"

"Carolwood." She lied. "Did you call the police?" She asked the question, knowing full well it was rhetorical.

"No ma'am. Sorry Hope; we can't call the police."

She involuntarily cringed.

"I know you're in pain. It looks like he broke your nose and you took a couple good shots to your cheek by the looks of it. Bear with me for a little while longer and I'll take you to the emergency room." He paused to consider something. "He didn't rape you did he?"

Before she could answer, the front door flung open. As if by magic, the short barrel .357 Dan Wesson revolver appeared in James's hand, hammer back, sights aligned on a trajectory with the center of Wes's chest.

"Jesus Christ! Wes," James shouted, lowering the weapon.

Hope watched in awe at how rapidly James had produced the weapon, and also, the fear on the face of the other man, whom she vaguely remembered.

"Sorry," Wes stammered, voice shaky and unsure.

"Not as sorry as you would have been if I'da' shot you!" James retorted. "Everything cool?"

"Yeah," Wes' voice still unsteady. "Jason's body is on the floor in the back. Clear outside. Nice shot by the way. You hit..."

"Put a lid on it Wes!" James cut him off. "Call Dave, tell him to get his ass out here. Alone! Tell him to bring a pair of Trish's shoes, jeans and a T-shirt." James again took his position at the window. How much more could possibly go wrong he wondered. He'd accomplished what he'd set out to do, but he sure hadn't planned to leave any witnesses behind. He shook his head in disbelief of his shitty luck.

From the threadbare sofa Hope studied the profile of the young man's face, a face that seemed troubled beyond its years, or the night's drama. Her memory of the event was returning in broken segments, however, she clearly remembered the bedroom door crashing in and Jason calling him James. But he hadn't offered his name. A lack of trust and well placed. She'd offered her name, her real name, not the undercover name she was using. A mistake made under the stress of the situation. She wondered again what he would do if he knew she was a D.E.A. agent.

"David's on the way." Wes announced entering the room. "Be here in five or ten minutes."

"Go get your truck Wes." James said, still studying the window.

Get your truck? From where, she wondered. It hadn't occurred to her that she hadn't heard anyone until they busted through the door. Why had they not driven up the driveway if they were coming here? Strange she thought, and yet, she couldn't think of a single reason to be close enough to this isolated house to hear the screams. Nothing but orange groves in every direction.

"Our rides here." James said turning away from the window.

Hope could see the glare of the headlights, dancing on the glass of the front window. She followed James through the rickety screen door into the darkness. The new arrival, "David" she assumed, met James at the broken down porch steps. He looked haggard and pale she thought, but also concerned about James. She wondered how James inspired such loyalty in people? He'd been barking commands to Wes, and now, David seemed ready to jump through hoops to do his bidding. He was clearly the field general.

"Hope, will you wait in the car? I'll be there in a minute." James said.

James and David watched her walk tentatively to the car.

"What's going on James?" David asked, when she was out of earshot.

"Long story Dave, but here's the short of it. Wes and I came here to kill Jason, found him in the process of raping Hope. I killed him to stop him." James let the words sink in then he continued. "Now I want you and Wes to burn this place to the ground, but before, you got to get rid of the body. Take it out to the Hopewell mines and bury it."

"What about her?" David asked when James finished speaking.

"I'm gonna take her to the hospital and drop her off. Did you bring the clothes?"

"They're on the passenger floorboard."

"Where's Trish?" James asked.

"Days Inn on Highway 60, room 217."

"Good man. Can you handle this?" James pointed at the house.

"I got it," David said. "Now get outta here."

Hope watched James walked to the car. He had a casualness about him she hadn't noticed before. She considered for the first time what he must be going through, how he felt; hell, he'd just killed a man. But whatever his thoughts or feelings he wore them well, kept them guarded. He had the appearance of one always in control.

"Should be some clothes by your feet." James said, closing the driver's door. "You want, you can change inside or you can change while I drive."

"I don't ever want to see this place again." She stated flatly, not concerned much about modesty, after all he'd dressed her a few minutes ago.

"Good enough."

She took a long last look at the rundown clapboard house as they pulled away. She couldn't help but wonder how long she'd be haunted by the memories of this house of horrors. "You knew Jason?" She asked, searching blindly for the clothes on the floor.

"Yeah, I knew him." He answered, turning onto the main road.

"How long?" She asked, pulling off her shirt.

"Most of my life, I guess." He shifted gears. "Always thought he was a little strange, now I just think he's a sick fuck. Excuse my language."

"Trust me he was definitely a sick fuck." She wiggled into the new shirt. "I'm lucky you showed up when you did, and the answer's no."

"No — what?" He gave a quick glance her way and turned onto the highway.

"You asked if he raped me." She said sliding off the shorts. "Answer's no. He was going to, said he was, but I think he got his jollies beating up on women."

"Well I'm just glad we got there before he hurt you any more than he did." His voice was sincere. He shifted again.

"How'd you happen to be out there anyway?" She slid the jeans on.

"Dog got loose."

"Hmmm. I guess I owe my life to a wayward dog." She leaned down to tie her shoes. "What's its name?"

"Uh." He stuttered. "George."

Gotcha, she thought. "So George it is!" She said, "I owe my life to a dog named George." Why was he lying? Where did he fall in the grand scheme of this case? One thing was for sure, there was trouble on the streets. This case had a deadly appetite for blood and it sure wasn't starving.

He stopped in the drop-off lane in front of the emergency room entrance. "Here," he said, digging in the right front pocket of his jeans. His hand came up with a thick fold of $100 bills. He snapped off the glittery gold clip that was locked around the bills and handed her the money.

She shook her head in adamant protest.

"Take the money," he said, "Pay for your treatment. And Hope..." His look was stern and unbending. "Forget everything that happened tonight."

She memorized his tag number when he drove away, leaving her at the curb, in God only knows whose clothes, with a fistful of money and a broken nose, that was no fault of his. She walked to a near payphone and punched in the emergency number.

"Hawthorne," his voice was groggy with sleep.

"Hawthorne, Brooks. I'm at the emergency room in Brandon and you better get down here..."

Chapter 10

Agent Hope Brooks was sitting, anxiously, on a cold concrete bench, when Hawthorne whipped to a stop by the curb. The seven-story structure, that was Brandon Humana Hospital, loomed behind her as she ambled painfully to the Crown Victoria. She winced in sharp pain, tugging the door open, the numbing effect of adrenaline had passed leaving her stiff and sore.

"You look like shit," Hawthorne said, "what the fuck happened?"

"Thanks," she said, "So do you."

He was a large man, an offensive line man in college. His hair was cut to a burr. His face, rounded by weight, was puffy with sleep, but his eyes were clear, she noticed. She gave him a play-by-play of the events that had transpired to the best of her, still cloudy, memory. He listened in silent disbelief occasionally taking a head cocking glance her way as he drove. When she finished her narrative, she tossed the money on the cream colored vinyl seat between them.

"How much," he asked, indicating the money with a quick head jerk.

"Sixty-three hundred and some change."

He whistled. "Now where do you think he got that kinda money just to give away?"

"We both know the answer to that question," she said, in answer. "But we can't prove it. What about the shooting?"

"We'll call in the locals," he said. "My guess is they're long gone with the body by now. We'll give the locals the tag number and your statement. They can take it from there; you're off the case."

"But," she said in protest. "I can get inside now! Besides, no jury in the world would convict him of the shooting, when they hear how it went down."

"Hmmm," he said, "you still want to do this?"

"Damn right! I've spent the last few months, in deep cover, trying to get in, now I have a way."

"Yeah, but now it's getting dangerous."

"Listen Hawthorne, whatever these guys are, they're not gonna hurt me. If they were gonna do that don't you think they would have done that tonight."

"You're probably right, but I still don't like it. I'll think about it and in the meantime you try to get some rest. I'm gonna set up a briefing with the locals for 10 AM. I'll expect you there." He dropped her off at her apartment, and watched her walk to the door, before he drove off into the small hours of the morning.

Inside the cramped three room apartment, Hope flounced down on the mauve pit group couch, snuggled up with an embroidered pillow, and for the second time, in more years than she could remember, cried. She wanted to go home to Alabama where she could be with family and friends. She had no illusions about how close she had come to death and she abhorred the fact that she was duty-bound to destroy the life of someone who had just saved hers. She gently prodded the puffiness of her bruised cheek, remembering the horrors that had caused the swelling. As a girl she dreamt of being a 'cop' and she chased that dream with the self-righteous determination to be the best, but at this moment she hated her job.

~ ~ ~

Miles away in room 217 at the Days Inn, Wes and David sat at a glass topped table, trimmed in dark wood, while James perched on the corner of the six drawer dresser. Trish lay under the coverlet, on the second of two double beds that took up most of the space in the room. She wasn't sure what the problem was but she knew that it was extremely serious. The somber moods of James, David and Wes spoke volumes in their silence.

[77]

"Trish," James said over the rattling hum of the air conditioner. "I want you to listen carefully to what I'm about to say. You have to make a decision," he turned to face her. His eyes, cold and hard, conveyed his seriousness. "These are your choices: you can take that," he pointed to the grayish-blue canvas tote bag lying on the otherwise empty bed. "And I'll sign the title of the Corvette over to you..."

"James I want —"

"Listen! Trish," he raised his voice to silence her interruption. "There's two hundred grand in the bag and I'll give you the 'vette and you can walk away, no hard feelings. But if you stay all decisions become mine; where you live, where you go, and what you do. And of course you never talk to the cops. If something happens, you only tell the cops your name and the name of an attorney I'll give you." When he finished speaking James looked at David and Wes. Both nodded their approval.

In answer to his ultimatum, Trish folded back the coverlet and stood up — pulling down the T-shirt she was wearing to cover her panties — walked over to where he sat, laced her fingers together and rested them on his shoulder for balance and kissed his cheek. "I choose you James," she whispered in his ear.

He snaked an arm around her slender waist, drawing her against him and shot a slick wink at David and Wes. "All right," he said. "Here's the deal. This ain't no democracy, it's a dictatorship, but considering my decisions affect us all, everyone gets to speak their piece. You first Dave"

Dave blushed slightly, but seemed not to notice. "I say, we head down south for a while," he said. "It's hot around here. I mean, three killings in a short time."

James felt Trish tense when she heard David's words. He tightened his hold on her reassuringly.

David continued, "Even if that woman, what's her name? Hope? Doesn't call the cops, a lot of people are gonna be wonderin' about where Jason is. So I say we set up shop in West Palm."

"Your turn Wes," James said.

"I agree with Dave," Wes started. "Except, I think we should learn from our mistakes here. See, too many folks know us and what we're doing here. So, I think if we are gonna sell in West Palm we should "set up shop", as Dave put it, someplace besides West Palm."

James nodded his agreement with Wes' logic. "Trish," he said, "You want to say anything?"

"Yeah. I like the beach." Her declaration got a good-natured chuckle from all three men.

"All right," James said after a moment. "This is the plan. I agree we need to distance ourselves from Keysville. Also I agree we need not *shit* in our own backyard. So Coco sounds good to me." He gave Trish a gentle squeeze. "We leave from here at first light. Wes you bring your truck, David you bring the ninja, and of course I get the beautiful blonde and the Corvette," he said, cocking his head at Trish.

~ ~ ~

The clock on the conference room wall read 10:12 AM when Mayhew rushed in. "Sorry I'm late," he said, dropping a thick lime-green file folder on the oblong mahogany table.

"I think you know Agent Brooks," the captain said to Mayhew. "This is lead Agent Hawthorne also from the D.E.A."

Mayhew shook Hawthorne's hand and glanced at Brooks noticing the futile attempt she had made at covering the bruise on her cheek with makeup.

"This," Hawthorne began, "is agent Brooks' statement," sliding a perfectly typed document to Mayhew, the Government insignia in the upper right corner. "This is what we propose," he continued. "You and agent Brooks worked together on this case. She's going to try to get inside and gather information about the homicides as well as the drug activity. She'll coordinate with you, and in return, you can share any knowledge you have on the suspects."

"Oh," Mayhew said, "I have plenty of knowledge about the suspects. I know all three; Griffin James, David Jones and Edmund Westhardt, quite well in fact. They've been raising hell in Keysville as far back as I can remember. But I'll be honest with you, I didn't figure them for murder. Also in my mind Griffin James should get a medal for last night's shooting based on agent Brooks statement." Mayhew raised the report he'd just read and cut his eyes to Hope Brooks. "You've made him sound like a hero. I was at the scene early this morning and I can tell you, the only evidence we have of the shooting is your statement. The house is now a smoldering pile of ash. I don't know for sure, but I don't think the body was in the house when they burnt it. Griffin James or 'James' – that's what everyone calls him – is pretty smart. Smart enough not to leave any physical evidence behind – hence, burning the house to the ground."

"What about the other murders?" Brooks asked, a little defensively.

"The way I see it," Mayhew said, "we're down to one murder. The murder of Warren Allison. Because, again, based on your report I'd venture to say we know who killed all those other woman and I don't think he'll kill again, because I don't believe in ghosts. The one I want is Dante Westhardt. He's the one behind the Allison/Westhardt murders. I can't prove it, but I know it, I've been doing this too long to be wrong about that."

The captain gave Mayhew a concerning nod, but more for the benefit of the agents. "What exactly do you want from us?" He asked Hawthorne.

"We want an A.P.B. put out on Griffin James, not to pick him up, but to intercept him, so we can set up a chance meeting between agent Brooks and James," Hawthorne answered. "Of course any information we uncover about the murders we'll share."

Chapter 11

"James," Trish said pointing at an enormous ultra-contemporary house resting amongst the sand dunes, with a realtor's sign stuck in the patchy brown grass of the front yard. They turned onto the sloped asphalt driveway. The morning sun was creeping into view above the multilevel, angular root of the sprawling gray, stucco structure.

"It's beautiful and right on the beach," Trish said. "Can we look at it?"

James was already punching the number from the sign into his cellular phone.

"Coast Realtors," a woman's voice said in the receiver.

"Yes ma'am," James said. "I'm on A1A 'bout 10 miles from Coco Beach and there's a great house with one of your signs in the front yard."

"Yes sir, I know the place."

"Good. The sign says it's for rent?"

"Oh, yes sir, it is."

"I'd like to look at it," James said.

"Okay, sir, when are you available?"

"How 'bout right now?"

"Well sir, we normally have to make an appointment. If —"

"I'll tell you what ma'am," James cut her off. "I'll give you $500 to show me the house right now, and rent it or not, you keep the money."

"I can be there in 15 minutes," the woman's voice said.

"I'm waiting," James said and broke the connection.

James and Trish were walking up from the beach when the new silver Town Car pulled in the drive. A thirty-something woman, with short frosted hair and wearing a dark gray skirt suit, greeted them at the front walk. She had a pleasant face and smile, shapely legs and a thin waist. They followed the woman who introduced herself as 'Carra' through the front door. The foyer floor had alternating black and white ceramic tile that reflected the light of the high chandelier. White carpeted stairs climbed the left wall to a suspended catwalk, that crossed above the lavishly furnished living room, that was five steps lower than the foyer, and off to the right. They continued forward until they came to an island kitchen, with a white tiled floor and black lacquered cabinets with white countertops and a breakfast bar. From there they moved into a dining room with gray marble floors, its east facing wall made of glass, offering a panoramic view of the sun rising above the Atlantic Ocean. They cut across the sunken living room, where James stopped to admire Sand sharks in an aquarium built into one wall. He caught up with the women on the stairs, and followed them across the catwalk to the master bedroom. The carpet here was also white and spongy thick. The ceiling, angled sharply, was mirrored and James caught Carra staring at Trish's reflection appraisingly.

James walked over to the side of the bed where Trish oblivious to Carra's appraisal, stood by the headboard and fiddled with the built-in stereo. Watching Carra's expression out of the corner of his eye, James snaked one arm around Trish's waste as his other hand slid up Trish's thigh bringing her short cotton dress with it.

"James.." Trish started to protest, but James silenced her with a `shhh'in her ear.

Carra, unable to stop herself watched as James raised Trish's dress with one hand and then ran the other hand down the front of her panties. Carra could feel the warm sensation of wetness spreading between her legs. It had been too long since she had had a sexual relationship of any kind. Thanks to a cheating husband, she had several rental properties and a thriving business, but in the aftermath of a nasty divorce, she had thrown herself into self-imposed exile away from any form of pleasure. However, she had been attracted to Trish from the moment she'd seen her, another oddity considering that she hadn't been attracted to a

[82]

woman since college, and then, her attraction only led to a single encounter between her roommate and herself.

James watched Carra's eyes travel up Trish's body as he slowly pulled the flower print cotton dress over her head and tossed it to the floor. With a sideward jerk of his head he encouraged Carra to join them as he ran his hands over Trish's bare breast and gently pinched her nipples.

Acting more reluctant than she felt Carra ambled up to Trish and James. Placing her hands on Trish's hips, she kissed Trish on the lips and was surprised at the passion in Trish's response. She could feel fingers undressing her, and caressing her, but she couldn't decipher how many hands were touching her, didn't care how many hands were touching her. It was about the moment, and at the moment she was consumed by the here and now. Her next conscious thought came when James entered her from behind. It almost startled her when the realization hit her. She tasted Trish's juices on her tongue, found herself between Trish's thighs, with James forcing himself ever deeper into her velvet depth.

She couldn't judge how much time had elapsed, twice Trish had reached climax at her urging and still James's thick member tested her depth, driving her ever closer to orgasm. When last she reached her peak and exploded into shutters, she drifted into the realm of ecstasy.

Sluggishly she returned to the physical world where Trish and James lay beside her on the thick white carpet each panting and exhausted. She couldn't believe she had just taken part in such an act, but yet she wasn't sorry, far from it.

~ ~ ~

"Mayhew," he barked into the receiver sloshing lukewarm coffee on his hands. *Fuck*, he mouth silently looking for something to wipe away the spilled coffee.

"Brooks," came a female voice over the line. "Any luck?"

"Nada," he said, finding a slightly used napkin. "James and Company seem to have disappeared without a trace. I told y'all he's pretty smart. He knows he left a witness, and although he doesn't know who you are he isn't taking any chances."

"Any suggestions?"

"Hmmm," Mayhew pondered the question. "Let me check with a friend of the D.M.V., they may be able to help.

"No idea where they might have went?"

"Could be anywhere by now, but one things for sure they're not in Keysville. I mean, I've practically had a constant surveillance on their homes, and nothing, night or day. As you know, that's a real small community out there, not a lot of places to hide. If they were there we'd know it."

"How's the rest of your investigation going?" She asked

"Same story, nothing new. I wish there was something we could do, but I just don't know what it would be. But hang in there, we'll find them. How you doing, anyway?"

"Still a little sore," she said touching her cheek. "I'd be a lot better if we could catch a break. This is always the worst part of this job, I mean the waiting game."

"I know what you mean."

"Keep me posted," she said and hung up. Damn! She hated this, she spent every waking hour thinking about this case, and considering she hadn't slept more than three hours on any given night since the shooting, she'd invested some serious thought into this case. When sleep did come, it was fitful and laced with dreams; always the same, a reenactment of that terrifying night, played over and over in her dream. The part that really bothered her though, was the fact that Griffin James had – in her dream – become her knight in shining armor. She hated that most of all. It went against everything she believed in. She had dedicated, and risked, her life to taking people like James off the streets. Drugs ruined people's lives and James seemed, to her, to be indifferent to the destruction he left in his wake. That, to her was unacceptable. It went against everything she stood for. It infuriated her that she couldn't hate him for what he was.

'I will,' she vowed to herself, *'bring him down.'* All she needed was a break. "God," she pleaded, "let me get inside." *'I can do this'* she told herself.

Chapter 12

Trish waited, apprehensively, on the black leather sofa of the beach house when she heard the motorcycles. She'd spent more than an hour preparing for this moment. Two hours ago James had called and said they were on their way home. It had been a long, lonely week in this big house alone. Oh, he had left her the Corvette and fifty thousand in cash, told her to spend it all if she so desired. But each day had been torture as she thought of her situation. She had agreed to spy on James for Russo, but only because she hadn't considered that she would fall for him. Now, he was always on her mind. She went to a local pick-up joint trying to break his trance and was rewarded with a few blatant offers and a couple groping hands, but in the end she drove back home, alone, wondering, where he was, and who he was with.

After he'd called she had showered and waxed. Then, standing in front of the full-length mirror in their bathroom she carefully studied her figure. Her thoughts drifted to Carra and the sexual encounter they'd had, and how jealous she'd felt of James. It didn't make sense. She'd never felt that way before; sex was a tool to her. She moved on to her makeup table and diligently worked her hair and makeup until both were perfect. Next she wiggled into the black leather shorts she had purchased for his return. When she finished tying the laces that bound the shorts snugly to her hips, she slid into the leather half-vest that laced up the front. Then she had waited – all the while telling herself that this was just a job. James was just a job.

She heard the garage door opening, the rev of the motorcycle engines as they waited on the door. She couldn't stand it; she dashed up the living room steps, nearly twisting her ankle in the spike heeled, black leather boots she wore. He was still straddling the motorcycle, pulling off his helmet, when she reached him, throwing her arms around his neck.

"Hey baby," he said, wrapping his arms around her slender waist, his still gloved hand on her hip. "I missed you too." He gave her a gentle squeeze and swatted her playfully on the ass. "Why don't you let me get off this thing and come inside."

She stepped back as he put the kickstand down and swung his leg over the seat. "New clothes?" He said holding her at arm's length. "I tip my hat to the designer 'cause he musta had you in mind when he made them."

She smiled shyly at his approval as he pulled a canvas bag out from under the cargo net that held it to the back of the seat. He draped an arm over her shoulder and led her inside.

"Come on boys," he hollered back to Dave and Wes. "I'm buying the beer." He tossed the bag on the couch; it landed heavily. "How was your week, baby?"

"Okay," she said, tears pooling in her eyes.

"Hey, what's with the tears," he asked, pulling a six pack and some chicken livers out of the refrigerator.

"Just happy to see you," she said, following him to the living room.

He set the beer on the coffee table and walked to the aquarium tossing the chicken liver to the Sand sharks. He watched the sharks attack the liver in a frenzy as he rinsed his gloves in the water and pulled them off. "Have you seen Carra this week?" He glanced in her direction to judge her reaction to his question.

She blushed. "Once, a couple days ago. She stopped by and we had lunch."

"Good, why don't you call her and ask her if she wants to go out tonight. Tell her that I've got someone I want her to meet."

Trish reached for the phone as David and Wes walked in from the garage. She punched numbers into the phone while the men guzzled beer and laughed at some event from the past week. After a short conversation she hung up. Carra will be here in an hour," Trish stated.

~ ~ ~

The club took up most of a city block. It was a single-story stucco structure, and judging by the long line out the front door it was a popular nightspot. James led Trish and Carra passed the line of would-be patrons with David and Wes a step behind them. He walked up to the man working the door. The man looked as though he could play middle linebacker with the National Football League. He had a fashionable ponytail and an angular face, twenty inch arms, and broad shoulders.

"Hey boss," James said to the linebacker. "Mick and Wayne invited us to come watch them play, they said I should give you this. "James handed the man a one hundred dollar bill.

"Right this way," said the linebacker, "and tell Mick and Wayne thanks for me." He led them to a table in front of the stage. "Y'all enjoy your evening."

"Who's Mick and Wayne?" Trish asked, as soon as they were seated.

"Oh," he explained, "The sign out front says Southern Comfort's playing here tonight. Mick's the lead singer, and Wayne's the drummer. They're a cover band and they're pretty good."

Their drinks had just arrived when the house lights went down. As it turned out Mick was short for Mickey; a petite brunette with flowing, waist length hair and a cute face dark bedroom eyes that sparkled in the stage lights. She wore a tight, sheer mauve top over her small firm breasts, her areolae dark and clear through the nearly transparent fabric. Her skirt was a deep purple, its end seam started high on her right hip, and raked sharply to her left knee where it met the fringe of her spiked heel leather boot. In the cascade of a powerfully bright spotlight, she strutted out to the stage edge. Another spotlight began to comb the crowd and her throaty voice, low and raspy, filled the club with opening bars of an old Warlock tune.

She was at the end of the first verse when she saw him seated at a table in the second row. She turned to her bandmates and ran a finger across her throat. When the music died down she called out to the technician sweeping the crowd with the spotlight. "Please light the fourth table in the second row for me."

The light swept through the crowded tables, everyone anxious to see the spectacle that promised to come.

Trish was shocked when the sharp overhead light flashed by, but then quickly returned to their table. The blinding white light lit their stunned faces as Mickey called to the crowd:

"I've got an old friend here tonight. How 'bout a nice round of applause for my friend James." The crowd roared in response. "Now I may need your help." Mickey stated when the cheers died down. "And he's gonna kill me for this, but James why don't you come up here and do a few songs with us?"

James shook his head, vehemently.

"Come on, James." Mickey called from the stage.

"Come-on-James," the crowd picked up the chant.

Cornered, seeing no way out, James started for the stage. The crowd cheered as James mouth the words *'You Bitch'* to Mickey.

A stagehand passed James a mic as he joined Mickey at the center stage. Again the crowd cheered as he kissed Mickey's cheek. The house lights went down and when the spotlight found the pair onstage they stood back-to-back.

Trish was amazed at the transformation in James. Gone was his normally stolid demeanor. Paired with Mickey, he transformed into a complete showman. The crowd clapped and cheered Mickey and James' performance wildly as they taunted, teased, and touched each other while they covered songs by Country, Pop, and Rock Bands. She especially enjoyed their rendition of Tina Turner's – *What's Love Got to Do with It* – even though she was slightly jealous at the way James stood behind Mickey, teasing, and stroking her from her breast to her crotch, as she sang about her pulse and the touch of his hand. She watched the duet act out the words of passion, pain, and love that they masterfully sang and harmonized about. They ended their show with the Gun -n- Roses ballad *November Rain* – one of Trish's favorites – and disappeared during a standing ovation.

A few minutes later, the linebacker showed up and told the group to follow him. They went down a narrow hall, of unpainted sheet rock, that ended at a flimsy wood door. Inside the cramped room, two men sat on a threadbare couch, another sat on a well-worn loveseat and against the far wall sat James in an armchair with Mickey propped up in his lap.

Trish and Carra casually strode to where James sat with a pleasant expression on his face. He extended his free hand to Trish, his other hand was wrapped around Mickey's slender shoulders. He pulled Trish into the unoccupied half of his lap.

"Who's the blonde with the great tits?" Mickey asked. "God, she's hot."

Trish blushed at the smaller woman's declaration.

"Back off Mick," James said playfully. "She's mine. Her name is Trish and Carra is her friend's name." James ruffled Mickey's hair "and this is Mick."

"How do you two know each other?" Carra asked.

"Your question James," Mickey said. "I'm too heartbroken to say the words." When she finally finished speaking she gave Carra and appraising look.

"Oh, you bitch," James shot back, stifling a chuckle. "If only you had a heart!" He patted her chest. "I was once a member of Southern Comfort, but I couldn't stand the competition. See, Mickey and I always fought over who got to take home the prettiest girl in the crowd."

"To the good Ole' days," Mickey said, draining her bottle. "Someone tell them to let the girls in. Let's get this party started," she yelled.

"I'm gonna skip the party Mick," James said. "Trish and I haven't seen each other in a week and I have needs."

"No fair James," Mickey said grabbing his crotch. "I can't compete with this."

"Where you staying?" James ignored Mickey's gesture. "Got an extra room at our place. If you want? Nice place on a private beach. You can ride with Dave and Wes. I'm certain they're staying for the party."

"I'm staying too, if it's okay." Carra said.

Chapter 13

Blurry eyed, James glanced at the clock: 5:36 AM.

"What is it James?" Trish asked in a groggy, sleep laced voice.

"Someone's at the door," he said, stepping into his jeans and grabbing his pistol off the headboard.

As if on cue, the front doorbell rang again. Alert now, James strode across the catwalk and down the stairs to the door. In the narrow view of the peep hole he saw Mickey with Carra by her side. Farther out the drive he saw the yellow light of a waiting taxicab. Pistol at his side, James unlocked the door. Swinging it open, he walked to the kitchen.

Mickey waved away the cab as she followed Carra and James to the kitchen. "Morning James."

"Uh-huh," he grunted, drinking orange juice from the carton.

"Since when did you start answering the door with a gun?" Mickey asked.

He looked at the .357 revolver in his hand but said nothing.

Mickey shrugged it off. "David and Wes were arrested," she said, offhandedly.

"For what?" He asked, shaking his head in disbelief. "When?"

"Assault and public intoxication." Carra answered, "'bout an hour ago."

"Fuck! Let me get dressed," he said in frustration. "Y'all wanna ride with me to bail them out?"

"Yeah, we'll go," Mickey said glancing at Carra.

"Thanks," he said, walking hurriedly back up the stairs.

Mickey was standing at the shark tank when he returned. "You're living pretty good these days James. What's this place cost you?"

"Thirty-five a month," Carra answered for him.

"Hell, that's more than I make. No wonder your girlfriend looks like she belongs on the pages of a Playboy centerfold." They walked into the garage. "Nice ride, classic ain't it? Can I drive?"

James tossed her the keys. "Try not to kill us between here and the bonds man office. I called Coco Bonds; their bail is twenty-five hundred a piece. Dude said he'd meet us at his office on A1A in twenty minutes."

"You know," Mickey said, pulling onto the four-lane highway. "I really enjoyed performing with you last night; reminded me of the old days. I intended to ask you to rejoin the band – pays a lot better these days – but not even close too enough to pay your rent. I won't bust your balls about your dealing, just be careful – you know how I feel about that."

"Yeah, I know Mick. I'm gonna retire real soon. Far as the band is concerned y'all don't need me. I mean, last night was fun but..." He trailed off, and Carra shifted around on his lap.

"What about your girlfriend, you love her?"

"Trish, she's a great girl. She makes me happy and she doesn't care what I do." He squeezed Carra's thigh. She blushed.

"You didn't answer the question James. You ain't, still thinking about Yvette are you?" Mickey caught Carra's guilty blush and shot James a knowing look.

"I bumped into her in West Palm a couple months back, spent the night with her. Then spent a couple of days with her earlier this week."

"Jesus Christ! James, you're an asshole! What about Trish? What's she think, for God's sake!" Mickey scolded.

"She knows, I mean she doesn't know who, just that there's someone else. I think Trish is pregnant too," he announced, shocking both Mickey and Carra.

"Oh that's great James," Mickey said sarcastically. "That changes everything. You're some piece of work. The poor girl is pregnant. For once in your life do the right-"

"Enough!" He cut her off in an icy voice. "I know it's fucked up but you know the family history. I'll probably die before the child is born."

"So stop dealing and get out of the business," she said, noticing Carra's confusion. "I care about you James and I wish you would let the past lie, all of it."

"I'm working on it Mickey, really." They turned into the nearly empty strip mall parking lot. The lone car in the lot was a dark blue four-door Ford Tempo parked in front of a single unit storefront that had the name 'Cocoa Bonds' painted on the tinted glass window. They parked next to the Tempo and went inside. The small office was sectioned off with two gray metal desks; each had a computer and a desk model phone. Behind the farthest from the door sat a squat, beady-eyed man with salt-and-pepper hair that appeared to have been trimmed with a steak knife.

"Morning folks. I'd say good morning but there's nothing good about being here first thing in the morning." He smiled at his own dry wit.

James walked to his desk and produced a stack of hundred dollar bills, in no mood for beady-eye's humor. "That's sixty-five hundred." He tossed the money on the cheap metal desk. "Five thousand for their bail, a thousand for your trouble, and five hundred I want you to give them when you pick them up."

"Wait a minute, I don't pick anyone up," the bondsman protested.

"Today you do. The way I see it you normally get 10%, and sign on for liability until they show up for court. I want you to post a cash bond, that I'm paying, that will be returned to you if they show up for court – plus the thousand I'm giving you today."

"Why not just bond them out yourself?"

"Let's just say I'm not fond of jails," James said, heading for the door. "Appreciate the help."

Astonished, Mickey didn't say anything but the look she shot Carra said it all. Carra shrugged off her look.

~ ~ ~

"I came as soon as I received your message. What's up?" Agent Brooks asked lead agent Hawthorne breathlessly.

"You got your break. David Jones and Edmund Westhardt were arrested in Cocoa Beach a few hours ago."

"Yes!" Brooks squealed in delight.

"Not so fast. We have some problems. The big guys think this is a little risky, and frankly, I agree with them," Hawthorne said, solemnly expressing his concerns. "The problem is not the chance meeting – we can cover you during that, but what happens after that?"

"Come on, Hawthorne," she protested. "You know this is the only way. We've been on this thing for months and we got nothing, nada, zip. I know the risks and I'm willing to take them – give me a chance."

"Hmmm," he grunted, pondering his thoughts. "We're out on a limb here and I'm telling you, one sign of danger, we pull the plug on this thing. That clear?"

"Yes sir, very."

Chapter 14

The glistening midmorning sun rays shimmered across the azure Atlantic water, up the stone path and spilled into the dining room through the east facing plate glass wall. At the dining room table sat Trish and Mickey sharing a breakfast of fresh fruit, toast and strong coffee.

"Do you really love him?" Mickey asked, referring to James and breaking the impending silence.

Trish, absentmindedly, drew up the collar of the black shirt she wore, and took in James' lingering scent. "Yeah, I love him," she answered earnestly, studying a vessel rocking on the distant horizon.

Mickey watched Trish, but failed to see the conviction in her words or her body language. "If it's any consolation, you're the only woman I've ever seen him spend more than two or three days with."

"You know a lot about him?" Trish asked, turning to face Mickey. "I mean about his past."

Caressing her bottom lip, Mickey pondered the question. "I know enough," she answered, bracing for the question she expected to come next.

"He's seeing another woman, Mickey. Someone in West Palm, from his past I think," Trish stated dryly.

"I know," Mickey said.

"He told you?" Trish asked.

"You have to understand Trish," Mickey answered defensively, but without malice. "James and I are very close, like lovers, but our love is friendship, always has been. Anyway, I was busting his balls about doing right by you, and he told me he'd bumped into Yvette. She's the only woman James has ever loved, and she broke his heart. He's never really recovered from that, it turned his heart to stone, and every time he starts developing feelings for a woman he splits for higher ground. That's why he left the band. He and I started getting real close, and he couldn't handle his emotions." Mickey's thoughts took her back, and she continued as though she was reliving the past. "James is unlike anyone you've ever met. He has a weird way of looking at things, but once you understand him you can't help but love him. He grows on you. His charm is natural and effortless, as too is his uncanny knack for seeing through people. James always keeps his word. My advice to you would be to let him get Yvette out of his system. He will, because he never forgives.

Trish turned her attention back to the rocking vessel riding the waves closer to shore. "People make mistakes," Trish said, bringing Mickey back from the past.

"Mistakes are one thing," Mickey said, "but if you betray James he will never forgive you. You have to understand what he considers betrayal. To him, lying is the only real form of betrayal. If the day ever comes that you win his heart it will forever be yours, but I'd say don't count on it, just enjoy what he gives you. James is hard, but fair, and he's fiercely loyal, until you betray him. But love is something James avoids."

"I'll never betray −" Trish's voice trailed off. The fifty foot trawler, gliding up to the dock, took command of her attention. "James," she whispered under her breath. Mickey was right about James growing on you but she had already betrayed him in more ways than one. Maybe Mickey was wrong, maybe he would forgive her. She met him on the dock, his hands slipped gently over her hips and firmly grasped her buttocks. She trembled involuntarily at his touch and tried to push the thoughts of her betrayal from her mind. He was here and she wanted to enjoy the time they shared together. She couldn't control the tears of guilt pooling in her eyes, she buried her face in his long, soft blonde hair and murmured the words of her only thought. "I love you, James."

"I know baby," he accepted her words and glanced at Mickey. "I'm a lucky man to have two beautiful women to come home to."

"Oh, James. " Trish whispered. "I look terrible, I just woke up. You should have called."

"And miss seeing you in a silk shirt and those cute skimpy panties – not on your life. What do you say we try out the bed in the Master stateroom?" He said lifting her bare feet off the slat planks of the wooden dock. She wound her slender, shapely legs around his hips, kissing him wantonly. She could feel the bulge of his hardness through the denim jeans, pressing urgently against the thin fabric of the panties covering the sensitive tender folds of her sex. She craved the intrusion of his thick length deep inside her and she blushed at the knowledge that she wouldn't care if he slammed her down on the hardwood planks of the dock, tore away her shirt and panties, and took his pleasure of her in front of Mickey and all the world. Hell, if Mickey wanted to join them that was okay too.

"Uh-hmmm," Mickey cleared her throat persistently. "If you two are done groping? I wanna see the boat."

Trish unwound herself from James, and he allowed her to slip through his grip until her feet were firmly back on the dock. His arm crept around her hip, his gentle fingers making stimulating circles on her flat stomach, as he led her to the trawler. "Have you girls been having fun while I was away?" Mickey slapped him playfully on the arm. "Okay," he said, "this is the Griffin." His voice took on a sales pitch tone.

"I thought you didn't like the name Griffin?" Trish asked, glancing in Mickey's direction.

"I don't like being called Griffin," he corrected. "But it's a fine name for a quality vessel such as this one. Right this way, ladies," he said leading the way to the upper deck cabin. "As you can see we have all the modern amenities; full-size fridge, range and of course, microwave. Notice the countertops and breakfast bar as we pass." James smiled in spite of himself, but continued. "Here we have dining room for six, complete with teak hand-carved table, and Captain's chairs. Next in the living room area we have a state of the art stereo system, HDTV, both a VCR and DVD player."

[98]

They descended a spiral staircase that ended in a long passageway where James continued his narrative. "To your left are two staterooms and crew quarters, to the right, here is the Master stateroom, note the plush thick carpet and mirrored walls. Here too, we have a state-of-the-art entertainment center. Walk-in closet to the left, and straight ahead a massive bed, trimmed in teak and polished brass, which brings us to the end of our tour. So Mickey if you'd be so kind as to close the door on your way out – I promised Trish a more intimate showing of the Master stateroom.

"Uh, well then I'll see myself out," Mickey feigned hurt, and stomped out closing the door in her wake.

"James that was rude," Trish elbowed him.

"You think that was rude? Wait'll you see what I have in mind for you," he said, something wicked, yet delightful dancing in his eyes.

~ ~ ~

"Sailor boy, that was amazing." Trish murmured, propping herself up on her elbow, entwining her leg in his, and stroking the rippled muscle of his stomach.

"You weren't half bad yourself, my little mermaid," he said, sliding his hand over her exposed breast, with exquisite tenderness. "You never said what you thought of the Griffin."

"Oh, I loved it before I was given your private tour, now I don't know how we lived without it. I never knew a boat could be so much fun tied to the dock."

"If you enjoyed that wait 'till I give you the encore tour at sea. I thought we'd take her out for the weekend. Maybe invite Mickey and Carra to spend a weekend at sea with us."

She could hardly concentrate with his fingers toying gently with her nipple. "Can't we go alone? I like Mickey and Carra, but I want to spend some time alone with you."

"Real soon Trish, be patient," he said.

"Do you still love Yvette?" She blurted out.

[99]

"Mickey needs to keep her mouth shut," he shot back, anger rising in his voice.

"Hey," she said in an attempt to still his anger. "Mickey loves you."

"Yeah, well love or not, Mickey needs to keep her big mouth shut."

"James calm down, I don't care."

"Oh, you care or you wouldn't have asked." He said, the anger subsiding in his tone. "Listen, I don't like answering to anyone about where I go or what I do. Isn't it enough that I take care of you and treat you with respect?"

"I'm sorry, James," she whispered, on the edge of tears.

"Don't be sorry. Just enjoy our time together and don't worry. I'll take care of you always."

"You promise, James?" She whispered, remembering Mickey's assurance that he kept his promises.

"Yeah, I promise," he said, giving her taut nipples a playful pinch, sending a shiver through her receptive body. "Come on, we have a lot of preparations to make; we need supplies for the weekend and I wanna get some fireworks."

~ ~ ~

"Damn honey, you'll have every bag boy at the Publixs trying to tote the groceries, dressed like that." James exclaimed, eyeing Trish in her cut off denim shorts and a halter top that did a poor job of covering her breasts. "Mick, the keys to the Vette are on the coffee table," he called out. "We'll be back in a couple of hours."

Trish followed James out the front door to the driver's side of Wes' four-wheel-drive. She eyed the high lifted truck suspiciously. "How do we get in the thing?"

James opened the driver's door. "Stand with your back to the truck." He put his hands on her hips. "Now on three jump and watch your head. Three!"

Trish jumped, ducking her head, and James lifted her easily onto the shoulder high seat. "Whew!" She squeaked in triumph. "Why so high, James?"

"For ground clearance in the mud and swamps," he answered, launching himself expertly onto the seat next to her.

"Can you drive this thing, James? I can't even see."

"Like a pro," he answered. "But if you're gonna sit next to me you have to spread your legs so I can shift."

"Sounds kinky to me." Trish said, spreading her legs to straddle the shift leaver.

"You never rode in a truck before?"

"Yeah, but I didn't have to spread my legs for the shifter, and it sure wasn't ten feet tall."

"Guess it's a redneck thing," he said, around a chuckle, as he navigated the monstrous truck out to the highway. "I love this song; *Major Moves* by Hank Jr."

"More of your redneck past?" She taunted.

"Watch what you say, it's all about a country boy who falls for a city girl." He squeezed her leg.

~ ~ ~

"Brooks take your position." Hawthorne said into the cellular phone. "We've got a visual on James. He and an unidentified female just left the beach house in a black step-side Chevy pickup. Damn thing looks like one of those monster trucks. I'll call back when they're headed your way."

"I'll be ready Hawthorne," Brooks said, exhilarated by the impending action.

Hawthorne found a space in the corner of the parking lot where he had a clear view of the black truck, and also, the front doors of the Publix grocery store. He watched James helped the leggy blonde out of the truck and disappear into the store. He marveled at how drug dealers, like James, seemed to have it all; pretty women to keep them warm at night, nice houses, fine cars and money to burn. But the glory was short-lived. If he had his say, James would have a six by nine prison cell, and a cellie named Bubba. A lot, he knew, hinged on Brooks, and not for the first time, he wondered if his plan would work. He still hadn't cleared his mind of all the potential faults of his plan. Brooks was basically on her own once she was inside, and despite her argument that these guys weren't dangerous, he was counting on the fact that once they knew she was a cop she was dead.

Hawthorne watched James and the blonde, followed by four bag boys pushing carts, exit the store. Must be having a party, he thought, as the boys loaded case after case of imported beer, and several bags of groceries into the truck. He saw James tip the young boys and then watched as they walked to a fireworks stand set up in the lot. After some time James collected a stray shopping cart, loaded his purchases and returned with the blonde to the truck. When they started driving for the parking lot exit, Hawthorne dialed Brooks' number into his phone.

"Brooks," she answered on the first ring.

"Subjects heading your way," he stated. "Get into position... And Brooks?"

"Yeah."

"Good luck."

"Thanks," Brooks said, already driving down the highway toward the beach house. Two miles from the house she pulled onto the shoulder of the road and shut off the motor. Quickly, she popped the fuse box cover and disconnected the wire the mechanic had pointed out to her. Then she attempted to restart the engine – nothing. So far – so good. She pulled the hood latch, climbed out of the car, and raised the hood. She took up a vantage point on the passenger side of the car. All she could do now was wait.

Just as the black four-wheel-drive came into view a car load of college boys slowed next to the car. She panicked.

"You need some help lady?" One of the college kids asked.

"Get the fuck outta here!" Brooks screamed, shocking the young man.

"Bitch!" He hollered back as the car sped away.

Brooks hardly had time to retort, so preoccupied was she at monitoring the progress of the four-wheel-drive. It was two hundred yards away now, – Showtime she thought silently. – She started to walk backwards her thumb in the air. She'd never hitchhiked in her life, but many times she'd seen people – mostly men – trying to catch a ride in this fashion.

The truck was close now, she could see his face – her heart skipped a beat – their eyes locked and for an instant she saw the recognition cross his features. Almost immediately, she heard the humming tires slow as he applied the brakes. She forced tears into her eyes and turned toward the truck, now parked on the shoulder. She crossed her arms over her chest in a self–hugging gesture and watched James leap down from the truck and stride toward her.

"Hope," he said, his brow creased in confusion. "What are you doing here?"

"M-my c-car broke d-down," she stuttered, through her gasping tears.

"No, what are you doing in Cocoa?" He asked, stopping in front of her.

"I c-came to s-see an old b-b-boyfriend we had a f-fight."

"Come here," he said, wrapping his strong arms around her back, holding her. "Shhh. It's all right, I live up the road, we'll go to my place and call someone to tow your car."

Yes! She wanted to scream, I'm in. Hope maintained the distraught façade, allowing James to help her into the truck. When they were back on the highway James introduced her to Trish. Hope's mind was reeling, there was still a mountain to climb, but at least she stood in its looming shadow. When they parked in front of the beach house she

[103]

waited until James helped Trish out of the truck, and then slid across the seat into his waiting hands.

"Trish," he said. "Hope and I will be inside in a minute."

Trish glanced at Hope, but obediently walked inside without a word.

"Hope," he said, when Trish was gone. "I don't want to hear one word about that night at Jason's, do you understand?"

"Uh-huh," she grunted

Satisfied he led her into the house...

James handed Hope a tumbler of Crown Royal. "Drink this, it will calm you down. Get comfortable," he cocked his head indicating she should sit on the black leather sofa. "And tell me what's going on."

Hopes eyes strayed from James to Trish, who sat on the loveseat. From there, to Mickey, who shared the couch, then back to James, who stood, with his back to her, watching the sand sharks. Reluctantly, she began. "For reasons I'd rather not say."

James spun to glare at Hope, firing a dangerous warning with his eyes. A warning that all three woman easily perceived, but only Hope understood.

"I had to get out of Tampa," Hope cautiously continued. "So I came over here to stay with an old boyfriend, but after a few days it was painfully apparent that things weren't working out. This morning we had a big fight. I left to cool off. Then my car broke down and from there you know the story." She sipped the whiskey when she finished, and waited.

"What's up with the boyfriend?" James asked, as he began to pace, considering her words.

"That's kind of personal," Hope responded.

James stopped in mid stride, his icy blue eyes boring through her. "Do you want my help?" He asked between gritted teeth.

Too terrified to speak, she nodded her desire for his assistance.

"Then answer the question," he ordered, his voice tight, eyes unyielding.

"It's over," Hope whispered. "I gotta find some place to stay."

James again began to pace, then abruptly stopped in front of Mickey and fished the thick knot of hundreds out of his right front pocket. He peeled twenty-five bills off the stack and passed them to Mickey. "Take the Vette and drive her," he pointed at Hope. "Back to her car to meet the tow truck. Have the car towed and repaired. I don't care what it costs. Then by her whatever she needs and bring her back here. She can stay in David's room at the top of the stairs. He won't be back for a while."

Mickey bobbed her head in understanding.

"James, everything I need is in my car. " Hope said.

"Do you have a swimsuit?" He asked.

"A swimsuit? No. Why?" Hope asked, not quite understanding the question.

"We're all spending the weekend on my boat. That includes you." He stated flatly.

"Oh, I don't know —"

"Hope," he cut her off, "it's my way or the highway. If you'd prefer, I'll give you some money and send you on your way, but that didn't seem to work last time. Just the same, the choice is yours to make."

Hope sat in silence, consciously aware of the stares of all present. "Okay James, your way," she said after some time. Mickey, see that her car is taken care of and make sure she has what she needs. If you need me, I'll be at the dock loading the supplies on the 'Griffin'," he said, walking out the front door.

All three women listened in silence to the sound of Wes' truck driving around the house and out to the beach.

"Mickey," Trish spoke first. "You two better be on your way before he really gets pissed."

"Come on, Hope; Trish is right," Mickey said. "Besides you and I need to talk about the right and wrong ways to handle James."

Trish nodded her approval of Mickey's statement as she watched the two women walk to the garage door and disappear. Then she followed the stone path down to the beach, where, still in a huff, James stacked cases of booze and bags of supplies from the bed of the truck onto the dock. He stopped after a few minutes, wiped the sweat from his brow on the back of his hand, and a shot her a quick half smile.

"James," Trish said softly, walking onto the dock. "Can I ask a question without pissin' you off?"

"Sure baby," he said, grabbing four cases of imported beer. "Walk with me."

"What was that all about?" She asked, picking up a sack of groceries and following him.

"Something's wrong here," he said, referring to Hope. "So I was establishing the ground rules."

When he'd set the stacked cases of beer on the boat's deck, she gave him a questioning look, then said, "Why bring her here?"

"Ah, because of an old adage my Grandmother used to say," he explained. "Grandma always said, you should keep your friends close, and potential enemies closer. Our paths crossed once before, and we got off to a bad start. My experience, when things start bad – they end bad."

"I understand," she whispered.

"Then let me do this my way, and don't take it personal because it's not." He moved back down to the dock for another armload of supplies.

"You know how much I love you?" She asked, when he returned with another stack of cases.

"I know baby," he set the stack down and brushed a stray lock of hair out of her eyes. "Just be patient, loyalty has its rewards."

Chapter 15

James sat on the balcony, enjoying the early evening breeze and the relaxing sound of the waves crashing against the beach. Deep in thought, he didn't realize Mickey was there until she spoke.

"James, do you want to talk about it?" She asked, startling him.

"Talk about what?"

"Come on James, I've known you too long" she sat on his knee, and rested her head on his shoulder. "Maybe I can help or are you still of the mind that it's you against the world?"

James drew a deep breath, and snaked his arm around her waist "Mick, you have known me too long."

"So out with it then."

"I don't know where to start Mick? I mean, things are happening that I don't understand and the people around me aren't what they seem, but I can't figure out what their motive might be for deceiving me."

"So you're still having a problem with trust?" She asked, cocking her head.

"It's not what you think, not like before, and I already told you that Trish says she's pregnant."

Mickey sat up and stared at James.

"I don't have to remind you of my family history, and I can't help but wonder if I'm making the same mistakes as my father and grandfather. Maybe the James family *is* cursed." He looked away.

"Do you love her James?"

"No." His answer was quick, and rang with truth. "It's not like it was with the Yvette or even with you for that matter."

"Gee, thanks."

"You know what I mean Mick," he said, pulling her closer. "Something's just not right with Trish..." He trailed off.

"And?" She asked.

"And Hope showing up here has the smell of foul play, but I have to figure out how to use it to my advantage."

Mickey pondered his words before speaking. "Where did you meet Hope?"

"I'd rather not say Mick."

"That bad?"

"More like, *what you don't know can't hurt you.*"

"You're a mess James and you'll never change," she snuggled into his chest. "But I love you and you'll figure it out."

"Why don't we run away and get married Mick?" He said playfully.

"Are you kidding? You'd be bored with me the day after our honeymoon." She kissed him on the cheek. "Besides I never could compete with Yvette's memory."

"Was it that bad before?"

"No James, it wasn't." Mickey stood up and turned to leave, James caught her hand.

"Thanks Mick," he said, smacking her ass. "Now you'd better go find Carra before she gets lonely."

The hours after Mickey left past slowly, but James was so engrossed in his thoughts that he didn't notice. One by one he considered the mounting number of problems he was facing. His life seemed to be spiraling out of his control and he didn't like that in the least. The question was, how could he gain control before things got so out of hand that he couldn't reverse the outcome.

It was well past midnight when James finally joined Trish in bed, but he hadn't spent the past few hours in vain, because now he had pondered his problems one at a time. As he slid between the sheets, he glanced at Trish's sleeping form and decided that he would address his concerns with her first.

The next morning James was up and gone with the sun. The resolve he had found the night before was his sole focus. After several stops, and many calls, he returned to the beach house to find Mickey preparing breakfast for Carra, Hope and Trish.

"Trish, I want to talk to you upstairs." James said, as he lay most of his mornings purchases on the dining room table, choosing to take only one bag upstairs, a bag from a local drugstore.

Wordlessly, Trish followed James to their bedroom; the other women stared in silence at James' somber mood. Trish also detected his sour mood, and her every step became more reluctant.

"In the bedroom" James ordered, as he ruffled through the bag he was holding.

"What's this all about James?" Trish demanded, with more conviction in her voice then she felt in her heart.

"Why don't you tell me?" He shot back.

"Tell you what?"

"Okay Trish, one last chance here. I want to know everything right now."

"What are you talking about James?"

"You ever use one of these?" He asked, tossing her a pregnancy test. James watched as Trish's mind registered what he'd tossed her, and tears welled up in her eyes, as her face paled.

"James I can —"

"Save it Trish," he cut her short with a sharp retort. "Betrayal is the final sin! I want you out of here, so pack your shit. You got ten minutes!" James stormed back downstairs and into the kitchen, where Mickey was finishing breakfast.

"Mick, I need a favor," he said, his voice low, but on the edge of fury. "Trish will be down in a moment and I want you to give her a ride to the airport." He dug in his pocket and came out with a wad of bills. "Give her this and drop her off," he said, handing Mickey the money.

"Is everything okay, James?" Mickey asked in disbelief.

"No, everything isn't okay, but I'm working on it," he replied, as he stormed out the back door.

~ ~ ~

Mickey found James sitting on the dock when she returned from the airport. She didn't know what she was going to say to him, but she knew that she wanted to comfort him. Also, she hoped she could get him to open up to her. They had been friends for a long time, and it pained her heart to see him this way. "James."

"Yeah Mick."

"You wanna talk about it?" Mickey asked softly.

"What's to talk about? Trish was lying about being pregnant, and I would have never suspected it, but this morning I searched her purse and found a phone that I didn't know she had, so I checked the messages, wrote down the number, and checked it out. Turns out, it was the cell number of my enemy. When I confronted her I knew she had betrayed me by her expression. So that's that."

"Why would she lie about being pregnant?" Mickey asked, with a puzzled expression.

"I don't really know, but my guess is that she thought I was going to leave her for Yvette." James paused, wondering how much he should tell Mickey. After a few minutes thought, he continued. "This is the problem Mick. Trish was feeding information to my enemies, and she could only pretend to be pregnant for a couple more months before it became obvious that she wasn't. Now, that only leads me to believe that my enemies intend to deal with me real soon."

"Deal with you? What's that supposed to mean?" Mickey asked, not really confused, but hoping she'd miss-understood his meaning.

[110]

"Don't worry Mick. It's my problem and I'll handle it." His answer was a vain attempt to still the troubled expression on Mickey's face, and the worried look in her eyes.

"So what about now?" Mickey asked.

"Now I wait to see what their next move is."

"Who are they James?"

"It doesn't really matter Mick, they're dangerous people, but so am I. If they want to play rough I can play rough too. If they're smart, they'll leave me alone if not..." He let his voice trail off.

"Just promise you'll be careful." Mickey said, concerned.

"Don't worry." James said, reassuringly. "Besides it's nothing."

Hope was standing in the kitchen, drinking a glass of orange juice, when Mickey and James came through the back door holding hands.

"So the trips off?" Asked Mickey, her disappointment clear.

"I'm afraid so, at least for now." James answered. "I'll make it up to you Mick."

"You bet your sweet ass you will, but I understand your situation, so go handle your business. I'll be here when you get time for me." Mickey crossed her arms and took up a defiant stance.

"You're all heart Mick." James kissed her cheek. "Watch for Hope; she can be a bitch."

Hope jumped at the sound of her name. She'd been so engrossed in her thoughts of the canceled trip that she had lost track of the conversation. "I-uh," she stammered "I kinda like her."

"That's right." Mickey called out to James as he left the kitchen. "We girls stick together."

"So we're not going out on the boat this weekend?" Hope inquired.

"No, something has come up." Mickey answered.

"Oh, is James upset about Trish leaving?"

Mickey leaned against the counter and contemplated her words before she spoke. "You don't really know James so let me try to explain him to you. You see, he had a bad experience with love once, and now he doesn't allow himself to become attached to anyone."

"He seems to be attached to you on some level."

"That's different." Mickey shuffled uncomfortably. "James and I are friends, albeit close friends, we're just friends. I'm here for James and I'll be whatever he needs."

"How is it that James inspires such loyalty?"

"That's easy – women love him and men fear him."

"Does that include you?"

"Does that include me what? Loving James?"

Hope nodded.

"That includes me, you, Carra, Trish, Yvette and any other woman he comes into contact with."

Hope was shaking her head. "I don't even know James. How could I love him?"

"Give it time Hope, just stand warned, James has an uncanny knack of seeing through to *who and what* people really are and what they're after. If you don't believe me, ask Carra how she met James and how fast he saw through her."

"But I thought Carra was your girlfriend?"

"James brought her here to me, because he knew I'd like her, and he knew I'd be good for Carra's self-esteem." Mickey locked eyes with Hope. "But just for the record, everyone around here is loyal to James *First* or they don't last."

Hope shivered involuntarily.

~ ~ ~

A few chaotic days passed before Hope had a chance to catch Carra alone. James had disappeared, but not before he strategically placed armed guards to patrol the property around the clock. Mickey and her band were back to performing a few nights a week at the club. It was one of those nights that Hope discovered an intoxicated Carra alone and talkative in the living room.

"Carra I've been meaning to talk to you." Hope said, after some small talk. "Can I ask you a question?"

"Shoot," Carra slurred over the rim of her whiskey tumbler.

"Well," Hope started, reluctantly unsure how to broach the subject. "I was talking to Mickey the other day – discussing James – and she told me I should ask you how you met him."

The flush on Carra's red-faced deepened, but the smile that crossed her glossed lips reached all the way to her hazy eyes. For a long moment Hope wondered if Carra was going to answer. Hope could tell the other woman was reliving the memory in her mind and Hope wasn't sure if she intended to share the occasion or keep it for herself. Then Carra's eyes cleared a bit and she began her narrative.

"You know I own this house." Hope nodded her affirmation. Carra continued. "Well I met Trish and James here to show them around." Carra paused, looking off into the middle distance. "From the moment I saw Trish, I couldn't keep my eyes off her. You see, she reminded me of an 'old friend' from my past. Not so much her looks – Trish was far more glamorous than my old friend, but they share the same mannerisms. I was transfixed by her, coming off a bad divorce, and lonely." Carra's gaze settled back on Hope. "James picked up on my desire for Trish, and initiated a sexual encounter. Looking back, I still don't believe the suddenness of it all, I barely knew their names, but it was what I needed on a lot of different levels. James knew that instinctively. As you know, we became friends and when James found Mick he hooked us up. Again his instincts told him we'd hit it off."

"How do you feel about James kicking Trish out?" Hope pried.

Carra pondered her answer before she spoke. "The truth is at first I was kind of pissed, but when Mickey told me the whole story I understood James' reasoning."

"What story is that?" Hope asked, intrigued.

"You better ask James, if he wants you to know he can tell you." Carra collected her glass. "Excuse me," she slurred, staggering slightly on her way up the stairs.

The silence Carra left in her wake was almost unbearable. Hope felt trapped and baffled by her situation. She had a job to do. For that reason, there was no way out and the more she found out about Griffin James, the more confused she became. Everyone spoke of him like he was some kind of Saint or the Second Coming of the Messiah. From where she was standing, it appeared to her that James had surrounded himself with a lot of desperate women that he used as his own personal harem.

The thought disgusted her and although she owed James her life, she too, knew that an evil man, at times, could be righteous.

~ ~ ~

Several uneventful weeks passed, with a frustrated Hope hardly laying eyes on James. Every eight or 10 days he would appear for a day or two, and then he'd be gone as quickly as he had come. Hope had used the many opportunities, where she'd been left alone, to search the house. But to no avail, search as she may, she never found anything of any significance.

One night, lying restless and awake on her bed, in the wee hours of the morning, she heard the revving sound of James' motorcycle coming up the driveway. A few minutes later she heard a commotion coming from the living room, and rushed out to the balcony to see what all the fuss was about. To her shock, James was slumped back on the sofa with Mickey perched over him barking orders to Carra and one of James' hired guards.

Hope, from her vantage point couldn't see what the problem was, but it was obvious that James was wounded and in a great deal of pain. Hurrying down the stairs, Hope's mind raced with all the possibilities. When she arrived at the scene she was surprised by all the blood, and James' pallor. He was clearly in shock.

With a dish towel and a bowl of warm water, that Carra had brought from the kitchen, Mickey began cleaning the wound in James' Lower left abdomen. With the blood gone, Hope could clearly see the bullet wound just above James's left hip.

"God damn you Griffin James!" Mickey scolded. Tears streaming down her face. "You need a doctor."

"No!" James said weakly. "Help me upstairs."

Hope watched Mickey and the guard struggle to help James up to his room. For what seemed hours Hope sat at the sofa, running the possibilities through her mind. She needed to contact Hawthorne, but didn't want to risk a trip out to make the connection.

"How is he?" Hope asked sometime later when Mickey finally came down from James' room.

"Honestly I don't know." Mickey answered, on the edge of tears. "He won't let me call a doctor. So we did what we could. We cleaned the wound and put him to bed. He's asleep at the moment. Carra's sitting with him, keeping an eye on his temperature. All we can do is wait."

~ ~ ~

Hope was reading next to James' bed two days later when he awoke from the delirium of his feverish dreams. For several moments she was unaware that he had regained consciousness. James used this time to gather his thoughts. What was Hope doing sitting next to his bed? Why did he feel so bad? As the haze lifted from his tangled mind, the events leading up to the shooting came back to him. The warehouse, the new customer, the intended double-cross – the gun battle... He needed to call Paul. He tried to sit up.

"James, you're awake!" Hope exclaimed, startled by his movement. "Don't try to get up, you're hurt."

'That's an understatement' James thought is a wave of nausea and pain wracked his weak body. "Get me a drink." He whispered, collapsing back onto the pillow. "Whiskey – bring the whole bottle." Hope, surprised by his request, considered protesting, but after a short pause thought better of it and left to do his bidding. She returned a short time later with Mickey in tow.

"James, honey you're awake!" Mickey exclaimed, bursting into the room. Clasping his face in her hands she lightly kissed his lips. "How do you feel?"

"Like shit." He gestured for Hope to hand him the bottle of whiskey. "Dial a number for me Mick." James took a long, shaky pull from the bottle before reciting the number.

"It's ringing," Mickey said, handing him the phone.

"Paul." James said after a moment

"Yeah – yeah, I'm okay." He paused, listening.

"No, – not 'till next week. I'm kinda indisposed at the moment." James shook his head and locked eyes with Hope across the room.

"The reason I called you is – you know that warehouse in West Palm? Yeah that's the one. I left a couple black canvas bags in the culvert out behind it. Would you go see if they're still there?"

James nodded his head for a moment. "Yeah, one is product, you can work that if you want. I'll get the other one next week. And Paul.... Be careful."

James handed the phone back to a fuming Mickey. "What?" He asked, as she slammed down the receiver.

"What *my ass*, James!" She turned her fiery gaze on him. "You damned well know what."

James caught Mickey's hand and pulled her down on the bed next to him oblivious to his obvious pain. "Shhh –" he whispered stroking her hair.

"I-I'm sc-scared." Mickey sobbed.

"It'll be okay Mick." James soothed, motioning Hope out of the room.

~ ~ ~

Hope would have liked to hear the rest of the conversation, but she'd heard enough to surmise that James had been shot in a drug deal gone bad. She felt slightly elated. After weeks of not even a hint of illicit activity, James had finally discussed his business in front of her. Was he beginning to trust her? Was it just a moment of indiscretion, a side effect of his present condition? Whatever it was, it was something to build on. The first nail in the Griffin James proverbial coffin.

~ ~ ~

A few days later, a blurry eyed Hope nearly bumped into James in the early morning hours, outside the upstairs bathroom door. James, returning from the kitchen with a fresh bottle of whiskey, staggered slightly in an attempt to avoid the near collision.

"Sorry. Didn't know you were up." James said his voice thick with booze.

"It's okay." She said sleepily. "I should have left the light on so it wasn't so dark. I'm glad to see you're feeling better." Hope said, in passing.

"Are you?" He asked. "I didn't know you cared."

"What's that supposed to mean?" Hope tried to shake off the sleepy daze in her mind.

"Well, I haven't seen much of you over the last few days." James stepped closer to her, trapping her against the wall.

"I didn't know you wanted to. It seemed that Mickey and Carra were taking up most of your time." Hope glanced at the closed door leading to James's bedroom, the only light in the hallway spilling from under the door, the faint giggle of Mickey and Cara's laughter the only sound.

"You could always join us."

"Not my kind party," Hope replied matter-of-factly. "But thanks anyway."

"Well, maybe, I could come join you?" James traced his fingers up her side, the thin fabric of her nightie doing little to shelter her from his touch.

"You're drunk James," she tried to push past him to no avail. "And I'm not sure that I'm what you want." She said, frustrated.

"The question is − what do you want?" James chuckled to himself. "But then, I already know the answer to that question." His fingers lightly brushed over her left breast. "What I don't know is how far are you willing to go to get what you want." James stumbled away laughing, leaving Hope to ponder her thoughts.

PART TWO

Six Months Later

Chapter 16

"Where's Mick and Carra?" James asked David, who was ambling up the dock arm in arm with a cute bleach blonde in cutoffs and a bikini top.

"Coming," David answered.

"Who's this?" James asked cocking an eyebrow at the blonde. "Flavor of the week?"

"Fuck you, James," David growled, turning to the bleach blonde he said, "don't pay him any mind Darla, he's just jealous." James laughed.

A few minutes later, Carra and Mickey appeared in the back door of the house and with Wes and his date in tow, they made their way to the *Griffin*.

"Nice boat," the brunette with Wes said climbing aboard, "I'm Debbie."

"James," he answered, "welcome aboard."

"Thanks for having us," Wes cut in, bringing a stop to James' open appraisal of Debbie."

"You two better get below and claim a room before they have you sleeping out here on the deck," James said climbing the external stairs to the bridge.

"Where we headed James," Mickey asked joining him on the bridge shortly after takeoff.

"An island a few hours down the coast."

"Oh, that sounds romantic."

"So its romance you want?" He said in a lusty voice.

"I don't know, James," Micky answered, fully understanding the innuendo. "It's been so long."

"Come on Mick, it'll be fun. Besides I'll let you drive."

"The boat looks like it's going fine by itself." She hesitated "what about the others?"

"I wasn't talking about the boat." He said with a mischievous smile, "and I wouldn't care if they watched."

"Is that your idea of romance?" She asked straddling his lap.

"What could be more romantic than passionate sex with the Captain on a beautiful yacht?"

"You're deplorable," she said, giggling.

~ ~ ~

Eight hours later, the sun just passed its zenith James piloted the *Griffin* through a deep channel of azure Atlantic water into a hidden code of a deserted island. The tropical palms and mangroves all but completely concealed the isolated paradise. The shimmering water of the quarter-mile wide cove was crystal clear and calm surrounded by sandy beaches as white as snow. At the cove's center, James engaged the switch to lower the heavy port side anchor and descended the stairs to join the rest of the group on deck.

Once on deck, James enlisted Wes' help, the two men quickly offloaded the motorized dinghy and a pair of Sea-Doo watercraft.

"All right ladies and Wes, James announced to a round of giggles at Wes' expense."This island is pretty small so it'll be hard to get lost, even for you Mickey." He pointed at her and got yet another wave of laughter. "But do be careful... Could be snakes."

"Only snake 'round here," Mickey cut him off. "Is in your pants and it's a harmless baby snake," she said getting cheers and howling laughter from the group.

"Is that right?" James shot back. "Why don't you come over here and I'll show you how it looks when it's a full grown snake!"

"James, Mickey." David interrupted their exchange. "Do you to mind discussing your sexual exploits later?"

Hope, who had been extremely nervous when the cruise started, was lightening up at the exchange. Again she was amazed at the fierce loyalty James inspired. Even to her, a total stranger, it was obvious that Mickey, Wes and David would stand by James thick or thin. The other three

[121]

women Darla, Debbie, and Carra she knew were just along for the ride. No matter what, she thought it should be an interesting weekend.

Hope road ashore in the dinghy with Carra, Mickey and James. While Wes and Debbie, raced David and Darla around the cove on the watercraft.

Once ashore Hope was content to sun herself on the beach as Carra, Mickey and James played in the chilly, calm water a few yards from the shore. This side of James she came to realize was a much different one then she had seen the night of the shooting.

The difference was night and day. Here he was all jokes and smiles – gone was the seriousness, strictly business attitude. He was caring, kind and thoughtful and more than a little amusing with his good natured sapient remarks. A glimpse of this carefree James helped her understand why his friends loved him, and she had to admit he was fun to be around and his wittiness was charming. She was lying on her stomach when his voice woke her.

"You coming back with us?"

"I must've dozed off." Hope said gathering her towel and T-shirt.

"By the look of your back you should have slept in the shade you've got a hell of a sunburn." He said. "I have some Lanicain lotion on the 'Griffin'; you are gonna need it."

"Ow I feel what you mean," she said sliding into her shirt.

When they were back on the *Griffin* Hope followed James below deck when he turned toward the bow and the Master Stateroom she turned towards the stern and her quarters. The boat was quiet and peaceful, everyone in their rooms resting from the day's activities Hope guessed. She'd been in her room about five minutes when a knock came to the door, but before she could answer James walked in.

She noticed for the first time his moderate, but yet powerful build. He didn't appear to have an ounce of fat on him. The walls seemed to sway as she remembered her dream. Panic was turning inside her.

"You okay Hope?" He asked in a voice soothing and calm. "You look kinda clammy."

"Too much sun, I think." She mumbled.

"Well, this will help," he held up a battle of Lanicain lotion. "How long have you lived in Florida?"

"Couple years," she chewed at an imaginary snag on her fingernail.

"Where'd you live before that?" He swung his eyes around the room as if he'd never seen it and then let his icy gaze settled back on her. "Alabama, if I had to guess based on your accent?"

"Good guess," she said, surprised at her own nervousness. "Sand Mountain," she lied.

He paused as if pondering her answer, absently biting his lower lip. "Lie down," he said pointing with the lotion bottle at the large bed in the center of the room.

Fear rippled through Hope as she glanced at the bed. His tone had left her unsure if his words were a request or a command. Despising him for her fear, she reluctantly walked to the bed. Her back to him, she slipped out of her cotton T-shirt wondering if he had detected the tremble that involuntarily swept through her. Lying down she braced herself against her thoughts of his intentions. She felt trapped, concerned. Was it safe to resist him? What would his reaction be? She shuddered and tightly closed her eyes as he untied the strings of her bikini top. His hands were gentle and slicked with the lotion when they began to whisper softly over the tender, sunburnt skin of her back leaving a cool sensation of relief in their wake.

"This will take care of the discomfort of the sunburn," his voice was as soft as his touch. "But you will be a little nauseous – sun sick – we call it." He gracefully retied her top careful not to draw the strings to taut for comfort. "Rest awhile and the sickness will pass." Then he was gone.

Left to her thoughts she abhorred his gentle kindness. He was after all the epitome of everything she despised even though the chivalry of his easy manner was in complete contrast to the ruthless world of contraband he so readily embraced. She would not allow herself to be seduced by his gallant charm. She made a conscious effort to steel her resolve. She had sworn a duty to protect the people of her country against the likes of Griffin James and she would perform her duties to the extent of her abilities...

Hope woke from yet another dream of James and as always he was dragging her out of the horrible grasp of some doomed fate.

She found her shirt in the near complete darkness. Shrugging into it she groggily made her way to the stairs. The *Griffin* was in total silence, her footfalls heavy and loud in the stillness as the craft swayed soothingly in the calm water of the cove. She plucked a candy bar from a crystal bowl on the breakfast bar and carried it outside to the stern rail. The night was warm but fresh and the stars sparkled in absolute darkness of the secluded island. She nibbled at the candy and admired the breathtaking vastness of the heavens.

"Beautiful night," James said, his voice barely a whisper.

Startled, she spun to find him silhouetted by the stars, standing at the rail above her by the external door leading to the bridge.

"Didn't mean to startle you. Come on up," his silhouetted form pointed at the stairs.

"Thought I was alone," she stumbled slightly on the stairs in the darkness.

His movement was quick and catlike. He seized her wrist. "Watch your step."

She immediately hated herself for her clumsiness, terribly conscious of his gentle but firm hold on her wrist as he stepped back to allow her passage onto the walk. He released her and she ambled to the rail before she spoke. "Been out here long?"

"Most of the night. It's peaceful, gives me time to think."

"About what?" The word slipped out before she could stop them.

"The future and the past," he said, sipping from a bottle of whiskey she hadn't noticed before.

"The past? What's to think about? You can't change it," she pressed.

"I wouldn't change it if I could," he answered. "The trials and triumphs of our past mold us into the people we are."

"So you're satisfied with who you are? Your accomplishments?"

"I'm satisfied that my actions were justified. If that's what you mean. I have no remorse or sympathy – people shouldn't prey on the powerless," he said, leaning on the rail next to her while offering her a bottle.

"That ideology is in direct contrast to the way you live isn't it?" She accepted the bottle.

"Is it? Why? Because I'm a *drug dealer*?"

His revelation stopped the bottle inches from her lips and sent a shiver through her.

"It's not the best kept secret in the world," he continued. "The fact I don't work, the way I live, anyone taking the time to notice could figure it out. But that doesn't make me a predator of the powerless, far from it. People have a choice; if they choose to let drugs destroy their lives, they have no one to blame but themselves.

"So you're perfectly willing to profit from their destructive nature?" She persisted knowing she was treading dangerous ground.

"Would you ask that same question to the bottler of that whiskey in your hand? I think not. What about the tobacco farmers?" He paused. "You see Hope, a lot of people have vices, but too, they have the right to choose. I simply make one choice possible. The government with their self-righteous prohibition, are the ones who've missed the boat, you see it's all about choice – a God-given choice."

"You're saying *God* gave you the right to sell drugs?" She exhaled in disbelief.

"I'm saying God gave me the right to choose. Another example God created a cliff on the north side of this island. If I jump off that cliff and plunged to my death, is God wrong for creating the cliff or for not saving me from my destructive nature?"

"God can't be wrong, because he's God," she said apprehensively. "But since you brought God into our little discussion, how about where He said obey His laws and the laws of the land?"

He stepped up behind her; she tensed as he grabbed the hand rail on either side of her, trapping her. He leaned close to her his chest against her back, his legs against hers and whispered in her ear. "God's law – how about the first commandment – thou shall not kill? Am I forever damned because I killed Jason? Well, that was my choice, even before I walked in on him trying to rape you." He felt her stop breathing. "He intended to kill me. I just beat him to the draw. However, even if I hadn't come there to kill him, I would never stand by and watch a monster like Jason take advantage of a woman. The nature of the contraband business at times calls for deadly extremes, but only those of us who made the conscious decision to play the games should be subjected to the fate we so willfully chance."

At the persistent burning in her chest she exhaled and drew a quick sharp breath. "But if I chose to play your so-called *games* Jason would have been justified?" She asked breathlessly.

"You miss my point Hope," he whispered trailing the feathery touch of his fingers up the side of her bare thigh, leaving goosebumps in their wake. "I don't agree with hurting a woman, no matter the circumstances, it's just not right." His hand slid under her shirt and rested on her flat stomach.

"What about Trish? Didn't you hurt her?"

"Trish betrayed me," he said flatly.

His wandering hand danced over her skin. Her world spun as sensation of his touch sent chills of pleasure through her receptive body. He slipped his fingers into the top of her bikini bottoms. She panicked. What was she doing? This situation was quickly getting out of hand. "James, I'm not ready," she forced the whispered words, not really wanting him to stop.

James withdrew his hand. "Let Jason go Hope. We can't change the past – your words not mine." He brushed a kiss behind her ear, hurried down the steps, dove over the rail and swam to the beach.

She could still feel the lingering of his touch on her skin. She put the bottle to her lips and took a long swallow. The heat of the liquor spreading like white hot liquid steel in her empty stomach. She wasn't sure what she'd hope to gain by pushing him into the conversation, but his explanation had caught her off guard. She could just make out the shape of the body lying on the sand of the beach. She wanted to turn away, but to her surprise she couldn't.

Whatever he is, she thought, he is a gentleman. That, she knew was no allusion and she had no doubt about the truth of his words. She carried the bottle back to her room and used her satellite phone to call Hawthorn. After reporting her location and well-being, she hung up and found solace in the numbing effect of the whiskey.

Chapter 17

The morning sun was just cresting the eastern horizon when Hope, squinting and groggy from the booze, ambled out on the deck. She wasn't surprised to see James leaning against the rail with a bottle of whiskey in his hand and by the smell of the smoke he'd exhaled she determined that his other hand held a joint.

"Mornin'," he uttered, his voice deep and whiskey coated.

"Morning." She arched her eyebrows. "Off to an early start?" She pointed at the whiskey and the reefer.

"Guess you could say that, 'cept I ain't been to sleep." His eyes traveled the length of her body. "Had some thinking to do."

"Oh," she said conscious of his scrutiny. "Want to talk about it?" She moved closer to him, his lustful desire was clear beneath the alcohol haze in his cobalt blue eyes.

"Talk's cheap," he stated dryly, blatantly exploring her curves with his eyes. "Besides, what good would it do me?"

Before she could answer, the laboring sound of an approaching engine disrupted the tranquil stillness of the peaceful morning. Affectionatelessly James grabbed Hopes hand, practically dragging her to the cabin door. Inside, he quickly turned to a built-in footlocker that she hadn't noticed before this moment. He fished a key from his pocket and jammed it into the Master Lock securing the locker door. Confused, Hope was unsure what she expected to see when he threw back the door, but she hadn't expected to see an arsenal.

"What the hell are you doing?" She screamed.

"Getting a gun," his voice was icy calm and devoid of its whiskey gruffness.

"Why?"

"Because that boat is coming in fast. Last night when I left you I walked around the island for a few hours and I saw that boat on the west side of the island. It came up with its lights shut off and sat bobbing against the horizon. I thought it strange then so I stayed up to see what they did. There are at least three people on that boat and they too, were up all night smoking cigarettes in the dark." He selected an AK-47. The weapon was loaded. Picking up a stack of loaded extra magazines he moved back toward the cabin door. Calling over his shoulder he said, "Get David, Wes and the girls up. Tell David I said if any shots are fired I want him to drive us out of this cove."

Shocked and unsure what to do, Hope watched James shoulder through the door and back out to the stern deck. His demeanor had changed instantly. One moment he'd been chiding playfully and the next he was all business, lethal but calm, cold and in complete control. She knew what he intended to do, but prayed she was wrong. The sound of automatic gunfire spurred her into action. The deafening report of the 7.62 rifle round rang out through the cove as the AK cut loose in a rapid succession of three round burst. She darted for the stairs. The sound of a smaller caliber weapon answered the challenge of the AK and the thud of bullets tearing fiberglass confirmed the intent of the shooter. She nearly collided with David on the stairs.

"What the fuck's going on?" David blared.

"They're shooting at us! James said for you to get us outta here fast!"

David raced up the stairs to man the bridge. Hope finished descending the steps to the lower deck hall where she met Wes and Mickey who, if reluctantly, were making their way for the stairs. The terror of the moment etched on their worried faces. Hope thought for the briefest of moments she detected the fresh smell of sweat, a byproduct of their fear.

~ ~ ~

James triggered the release and the spent magazine tumbled to the deck joining the brass shell casings that lie askew at his feet. With a practiced dexterity he jammed another clip home and was rewarded by the mechanical shift and clang of the weapons' bolt snapping forward locking a fresh round in the firing chamber.

The invading vessel – a thirty foot Fly Bridge – was circling. James held no illusions as to the intent of the Fly Bridge crew if the fact that they'd anchored just off the island in the small hours and never so much as used a flashlight wasn't enough to convince him. No one in their right mind on a pleasure cruise or fishing expedition would navigate the inlet channel at the rate of speed at which they'd approached. So it really came as no surprise to James when the brazen Latino on the aft deck raised the Uzi he held cradled in his hands, and pointed it in James's direction.

Surprise this day, however belonged to James. When he'd seen the Fly Bridge arrive in the wee hours, bobbing on the sporadic rhythm of the Atlantic swells, he had a gut wrenching feeling it would come to this. He'd swum back to the *Griffin* half expecting to find Hope sitting silently in the shadows of the nights' stillness. After a quick search of the common deck and the bridge turned up no one, he determined Hope must have returned to her quarters. He grabbed a bottle of Single Barrel Jack from the liquor cabinet and after injecting a heavy dose of his powerful meth he slipped out of the cabin to listen, watch and wait. He passed the wee hours sipping his Jack and pondering his future; his alcohol and drug abuse weighed heavy on his altered mind. Then his thoughts drifted to Hope. There was something about her, but how was he going to bridge the distance that separated them?"

~ ~ ~

The Latino occupants of the Fly Bridge were intent on surprising them, but they had made a fatal error in judgment. No hunter should ever underestimate his prey. As the Latino slowly raise the Uzi, James, with controlled three-round bursts, peppered the attacking vessel, until the slide of the AK locked back signifying that the clip was empty.

The Latino's first shots came as James exchanged the empty clip for a full magazine. James heard the dull thud of the 9 mm Uzi rounds punching holes in the *Griffin's* hull, but fear was not an option, the lives of everyone on board rested squarely on James's shoulders and no matter what, he'd be damned if he'd let his friends down. Standing, like a madman with a death wish, as the onslaught of 9 mm rounds whistled all around him, James unleashed his fully automatic AK spraying down the deck of the Fly Bridge. His action sent the opposing captain sailing over the side and left the Fly Bridge on a crash course with a cliff of solid rock at the cove's edge. James bolted for the cover of the cabin, but before he could make the door he felt the 9 mm round spin a burning furl through his left arm. Pain rifled through him as he dove for cover on the deck.

"Stay down!" Hope shouted in a voice that was tempered with control and determination.

"What about James?" Mickey asked, tears streaming down her cheeks leaving glistening wet trails that shimmered in the pale light of the hallways globed light fixtures.

"He'll be all right." Hope answered, her words more confident than she felt in her heart. At that moment she knew Griffin James had stolen her heart and a powerful need to protect him washed over Hope. In a futile attempt to return to the main deck she made the third step before the ear shattering explosion nearly capsized the *Griffin.* The unexpected bone jarring jerk flung her over the small rail crumpling her in a heap of sharp agonizing pain on the floor. Carra, who just entered the hall before the explosion, lay in a heap with Mickey.

In a vain attempt, Hope struggled against the darkness, fighting for a foothold. Darkness engulfed her consciousness. The hallway walls appeared to be breathing. Mickey and Carra swam in and out of focus. Hope's every nerve-ending registered sharp wracking pain forcing her to choke back nauseous bile. She was barely aware of the droning vibration of the engines taking hold, but when the shuddering of drive lines being engaged rippled through the fiberglass hall, another acute wave of pain wracked her battered senses, the darkness swept in encompassing her in its inky blackness.

By the time Carra and Mickey had fought off the lingering effects of the early morning surprise attack, Darla and Debbie had joined them in the close confines of the cramped passage. Working together the four women dragged more than carried Hope to the Master state-room and placed her on the enormous platform bed that occupied the room's center.

Mickey was in the process of cleaning the rivulets of bright red blood that trickled out of Hopes battered nose when James appeared in the doorway. Involuntarily, Mickey shrieked back at the sight of him. In his right hand he held the assault rifle. He was shirtless and blood cascaded from a nasty looking quarter size hole in his left bicep creating velvety pools of shimmering red fluid on the thick carpet. But it was the look in his eyes that caused Mickey to backpedal a step. His face was contorted in a sinister menace and his eyes were an evil sanctuary of lethal carnage. His skin was pale and chalky covered in a slick sheen of sweat.

"Prop her head up and let her nose drain or you'll black her eyes," his words were a blunt clamor and spoke with great effort. Mickey nodded her understanding, but James missed the silent affirmation as he fell sprawling to the floor, his consciousness slipping away.

~ ~ ~

The sparkling light of day was waning on the distant horizon through the star board portal when consciousness reclaimed him, he felt weak and throbbing pain searched through his left shoulder, up his neck, announcing its sickening presence like a morbid explosion to his awareness. Between the pulses of pain his memory returned in waves of the power known only to those who have endured live fire gun-battles at the peril of their own life. He searched the shadows of the Master stateroom for signs of life and for a moment thought himself alone until his wandering gaze settled on the covered form of a woman who shared the huge bed with him. He let his eyes drift over her generous curves covered but not disguised by the sheet. When his appraising eyes reached Hope's face he found her returning his stare in the failing light.

"Well?" She asked abruptly.

"Well what?" He shot back.

"Well, do you like what you see? Or should I throw back the covers so you can get a better look?" She answered defiantly in a contemptuous tone.

With a swiftness that defied his condition he rolled over to his right side to face her and snaked his wounded left arm around her thin waist drawing her tight against him. His movements came at a price, one he paid with a shudder of pain. He ground his teeth against the urge to groan at the sharp intrusion of pain. No matter the severity of his torment he wouldn't give her the satisfaction of seeing him in a weakened state. On the other hand his swiftness had caught her off guard, startled surprise had her brows arched and her eyes wide in alarm. He felt her sudden intake of breath as her firm breast collided with his bare chest, only the thin fabric of her cotton shirt separated them from shoulder to waste. Their lips so close that they were forced to share the air that they drew life's sustaining breath from. His eyes bore his challenge into her daring her to back down from his flagrant advances toward coitus.

[133]

For all his roughness she knew all she needed to do was tell him to stop but conflicting messages were congregating in her brain. Each fighting to be heard. Her body was pleading to let him have his way. Her nipples had instantly swollen to a painful firmness and a warm wetness was seeping from the tender folds between her thighs. It had been far too long since she had accepted a man – almost two years – and the physical-ness of his touch combined with the taboo of an encounter with him had her senses spiraling out of control. She needed to resist the temptation of the pleasure he offered her, but her resolve had fled, leaving her wanting him.

He flipped onto his back dragging her on top of him. She could feel the bulge of his manhood and his masculine muscular fingers felt electric gliding over the convex-ness of her buttocks. She closed her eyes as his fingers slid under the satiny fabric of her panties and danced and untamed concupiscent waltz over her nether region. The sinful gratification of his tantalizing touch forbade reason and enticed her to bend to his will. Too long, she told herself, making excuses for her wanton lust. Her love for him was in complete contrast to the carnal desire he inspired in her. But he was, after all, her knight in shining armor and for all his faults his uninhibited sensual touch was an exhilaration driving her precariously close to a sexual bliss unlike any she'd known. The feathery touch of his tongue's tip traced her throat from the base of her neck over her quivering chin and compelled her to part her trembling lips allowing his tongue to invade her mouth.

She surrendered herself to his every whim, content to let him guide her. Not like she had a choice – so long as his masterfully skilled fingers coaxed her, she was his marionette and she would sway to any symphony his touch commanded. The cadence of his caress marched her toward crescendo; the tempo of her shoulders denoted her impending climax as did her sporadic breathing. She tensed. Relaxed. Tensed and fell into the convulsive grasp of

[134]

orgasmic revelation. Her grasp on reality faltered and the upward spiral of pleasure swept her into the oblivion of sweet release to celestial heights far exceeding any she'd ever reached or aspired to attain.

Slowly the heavenly sanctuary of boundless sexual bliss with its radiant pleasure, faded. Then the copiously rich experience overwhelmed her to tears. She quickly averted her eyes from his piercing gaze, embarrassed by her tears. The spiritual intimacy of what he did next confirmed to her that she was way out of her league – he cradled her head and pulled her face into the crook of his shoulder, held her tight, and let her cry the soul healing tears of salvation.

"I'm s-sorry," she stuttered through her tears, her voice laden with the emotion of the experience and heartfelt love.

"Don't be," he cooed, his voice soft and seductive. He pushed a tear soaked auburn lock of hair from her face. "Everybody needs somebody sometime."

"But you don't understand –"

"Shhh," he cut her off. "I understand more than you think."

She fixed him with a questioning stare. Did he know? His words had caught her off guard. His eyes had softened a bit, but still held the steely edge that unnerved her and anyone he pinned them with. She charged on despite the flashing red warning sign going off in her mind. "Where do you turn when you need someone?" She asked, her secret still safe, she hoped?

"I'm the exception not the rule," he stated, around his cocky half grin. "I'm a loner by choice; life's easier that way. I chose to be on top and it's lonely on the top. That's part of the game. The game is hard, and often cruel at times, but it's fair."

"Is that your explanation for what happened this morning? Just another part of the game?"

He cocked his head and arched his brow taken aback by her frankness. "This morning was a retaliation because I killed Jason. Now they can add three more bodies to their list of failures."

"Did you kill them?"

"I shot two of them, the third was still on the boat when it exploded. He's the bastard that shot me."

She gently fingered the bandage on his left arm. "Does it hurt?"

It's mind over matter," he chuckled. "What I don't mind, just doesn't matter."

"What are you gonna do now?"

"I told Dave to take us to Grand Bahama before I came down to check on you and passed out. You and the girls will be safe there until I can handle this little problem." He raked a hand through her silky hair as he announced his plan. "I will rent y'all a place and buy you everything you need."

Hopes mind reeled with the dilemma of her situation and the words were out before she could stop them. "Can't I stay with you?" The problem was, her words were a desire to be with him, and not out of duty.

He shook his head in amusement. "I think that bump you took on the head is affecting your judgment. People are trying to kill me and they won't think twice about killing you if you're with me. Don't panic I'll have it taken care of in a few days."

"And how's that," she demanded.

"I figure if you want to kill the snake it's best to cut its head off."

She tensed at the meaning of his words. "Cut off as many heads as you want to. I'm going with you." She shot back her words filled with determination.

"Suit yourself." He rolled her off him and slid off the bed. "But don't say I didn't warn you." He cupped her breast with his hand and stroked her nipple through her shirt with his thumb. "Might be fun though — maybe I can find time between shootouts to finish what we started." With that he strode out of the room leaving her to her thoughts.

She couldn't believe she'd allowed him to touch her and worse yet was the fact that he had left her wanting more. The fire he'd ignited in her still smoldered in his wake and threatened to burn out of control. Who's fooling who she wondered.

Chapter 18

The colossal three-story mansion of tinted glass shimmered like a massive diamond in the carefully aimed light beams that masterfully illuminated the landscape in the dead of night. Armed guards with huge attack dogs patrolled the shadows of the secluded tropical paradise fortress.

James was impressed with Paul's attention to security as well as his taste in lodging. When he'd called Paul on his satellite phone to ask for Paul's assistance in securing a safe place for the girls, he'd hardly expected this. The place was fit for a queen – by the looks of it – and guarded like Fort Knox. In short it was perfect, and the fact that David and Wes could fly back to Florida from here put them one step closer to carrying out his plan. A plan, that had David, Wes, Hope and himself returning to Keysville to settle the score once and for all.

From his vantage point on the *Griffin's* control deck he could see Paul waiting on the brightly lit dock. After maneuvering the seagoing vessel tight against the pylons he turned to face Mickey who occupied the copilot's seat. The silence between them was loud and threatening. He knew she was upset about being abandoned on the Bahama Island, but too, James knew that it was the safest place for her at the moment.

"Don't go James," she pleaded her bottom lip quivering.

"I have to," he said through clenched jaws. "You have to trust my judgment Mickey – you'll be safe here and I'll be back in a few weeks."

She turned to hide her tears. "I'm scared James. We may never be more than friends, but God dammit I love you!"

"Mickey," James wrapped his arms around her in a vain attempt to comfort her. "Not now baby." He guided her down to the main deck and out to the dock where Wes and

Dave were at the task of offloading the luggage. Darla and Debbie stood off to one side next to a fidgeting Carra. Hope sat perched on the transom. Paul barked orders to a group of guards. The atmosphere was somber at best — everyone seemingly content with the silence.

"That's everything," David said, placing the last armload of baggage on the wood slats of the dock.

James nodded. "Where's my end of the last load of dope?"

David pointed at a canvas bag lying on the stern deck of the *Griffin*.

"How much is it?" James questioned snatching up the heavy duffel bag.

"One-point-two," Paul answered reluctantly as all eyes in hearing distance snapped in his direction.

"You're a loyal friend Paul and the past year you've made me wealthy," James tossed the bag of money at Paul's feet. "See that everyone has what they need and if something happens to me give whatever is left to Mickey." He felt Mickey go rigid as he kissed her tear stained cheek. "You have been a loyal friend. I love you too Mick." His whispered words caressed her ear.

Carra crossed the deck to wear Mickey and James stood. Taking Mickey's trembling hand. "Come on honey," she encouraged Mickey flipping James a quick shy glance.

James turned to face Paul. "Thanks, I owe you one."

Paul shook his head in understanding.

James turned to David and Wes. "I want you two to fly back to Tampa and wait someplace safe for me to call you. It will probably be in a week, maybe ten days.

"Where are you headed?" Wes asked very cautiously.

"The beach house in Cocoa," James answered flatly.

"What about her?" David snidely cocking his head toward Hope.

"She's with me," James fired back.

"That's not real smart James," David declared not willing to concede his point of view.

"Oh no!" James exploded. His face contorted instantly in rage, his eyes a blazing inferno. "Why, because she might hear something or see something she shouldn't? It's far too late for that. In case you forgot she saw me blow Jason's fuckin' head off! So don't tell me what's smart. I run this show! It's my recipe that makes the money and my smokin' gun that keeps us all alive. Do you understand that?"

Hope watched the exchange from the boat. She had never seen him this angry and didn't care to ever see it again. Even in the semi darkness she could see him trembling in fury, on the edge of out of control, his face backlit by the landscape light was a pure mask of fury.

David shrieked back. "All right James." He raised his hands defensively, surprised by James's outrage.

James took a couple deep breaths in an attempt to calm himself. "Sorry Dave. It's been a rough weekend." He rubbed his wounded left arm absently. "Listen, it was Russo's people that attacked us."

"Are you sure?" Wes asked in disbelief.

"Yeah, I'm sure. They were Cuban or Puerto Rican or something and the way I see it Dante hired them through Russo. What I can't figure out is how they found us on a deserted island in the Atlantic Ocean." James combed his fingers through his hair, "Someone had to call them in."

"Someone on the boat?" David asked baffled.

"No one knew where we were going until we were on the boat and I watched the radar. No one followed us." James stated.

"Who?" Wes asked, looking at Hope.

"No," James said following Wes's eyes. "She's the only one that I know for a fact that didn't have access to the radio. She was on the beach all day. Then asleep in her room until late. When I left the boat I swam to the island and saw the other boat."

Hope expelled a sigh of relief. James was right about her, but then who called in the assassins? Hawthorn? Her boss? Was he dirty? How could her situation get any more out of hand? And why had James lied to protect her?

"Wes, are you in?" James asked.

Wes knew exactly what James was asking, he had no illusions as to James' intentions. His uncle Dante was a marked man and for once Wes didn't envy his uncle. Wes knew James had an uncanny knack for rising to the top of the heap. "I'm in."

James nodded his approval of Wes's loyalty. "For the record I'll pull the trigger – right after I get some answers from him. I don't expect you to do that Wes." James took Hopes hand and led her to the stairs. "I need some sleep, I leave at first light."

"She gonna help you sleep?" David hooted with a chuckle as they descended the steps.

Hope felt the heat of embarrassment race up her neck and settle on her cheeks. Thankfully it was dark enough no one could see her blush, but bewitched by the dilemma of what lay ahead. She was supposed to be gathering evidence against him and the conversation she'd just heard was enlightening, but her problems started where duty stopped and desire started. Her resolve to bring him down was faltering because of the strength and tenderness she had found in his bloodstained hands. He was a murderer, but he didn't kill indiscriminately or without reason. Yet how could she condone his plot of vengeance and murder?

The soft glow of the corner mounted globes cast seductive illumination on the leopard patterned coverlet. The sensual sound of a survivor tune about a trembling touch and the hand of fate whispered its seduction from the headboard mounted player and the carnal desire flickered like an open fire in his eyes. She couldn't remember the last time or even if there had ever been a time when a man had look at her in such a primal way. Better judgment shouted at her, demanding she make a stand and resist him, but the shouts were drowning in the persistent pound of her accelerated heartbeat.

He tangled his fist in her hair and tilted her head back, his eyes penetrated her. With his thumbs he traced her cheekbones down to the corner of her mouth and across her trembling bottom lip until they met at its full creased center. His touch was tantalizing as his thumb drifted to her chin and along her jawline. His fingers danced down her graceful neck and over her lightly freckled chest to the top button of her low-cut blouse. With a deliberate slowness he unfastened the bindings of the blouse and slid it off her shoulders. Her breast rose and fell as she gulped air in anticipation. He hooked his thumbs in the elastic waistband of her cotton shorts pushing them over her pleasantly ample hips and allowing them to cascade to the floor. She closed her eyes as he un-clasp her frilly strapless bra and a shiver rippled through her as he slid her scanty laced panties down her thigh.

"Open your eyes Hope," his voice was gruff and heavy with desire.

She obeyed his command and with the same rate of deliberation he shed his slingshot style tank top revealing the bunched wave of muscles on his stomach, shadowed by his sharply convex muscular chest. He unfastened the button up fly of his Levi's jeans and pushed the jean along with his silk boxers to the floor. The length of his manhood was thick and erect, but it was his casual brashness that had enraptured and transfixed.

He too took advantage of the opportunity to admire her. The way her auburn hair framed her classic Anglo features; high cheekbones, emerald eyes, a petite nose, pouty lips, a sharp jawline in narrow cleft chin. Her normally alabaster skin still brightly burned from the sun except for the triangle patches where her bikini had covered her firm, ample breasts. The fine, neatly trimmed auburn down arching from between her thighs was framed by alabaster skin untouched by the suns violent rays.

Time past, but how much she would never know. Again and again he took her past the point where she was certain it was impossible to reach. Then each time he set a new height, he changed his approach and carried her higher, until he took her to a plane of physical and spiritual redemption; a celestial sanctuary, a heavenly realm of emotional salvation and awareness. Lying in his arms, spent from the physical exhilaration of offering herself completely, she slept the sleep of the dead. A sleep, devoid of dreams, induced by exhaustion, so deep that time and place ceased to exist.

"Hope..."

Her name drifted through the inky blackness and caressed her skin like a warm mid-summer zephyr. She resisted the temptation to answer the seductive voice beckoning to her.

"Hope..." The voice persisted with its velvety softness.

Again the sensation danced on her skin stroking her sensitive nerve endings to a state of heightened awareness. Reluctantly she surrendered to the voice and spiraled toward the light of consciousness, abandoning the darkness of fathomless slumber.

The Master Stateroom was cast in shadow; it's only light provided by the port and starboard portals. Her eyes searched the room in confusion. Her mind still trapped in the haze of sleep. Reality slowly asserted itself and as understanding set and she found him seated next to her.

"Mornin' sunshine." James whispered, stroking the contour of her hip through the satin sheet. "Sleep well?"

"God, did I," she answered, clutching the sheet in both hands "what did you do to me?"

His lips curled in a half smile "I just done what came natural — it takes two." He pushed a wild lock of auburn hair off her cheek. "You may want to shower and dress. We have a busy day ahead of us. Wear something casual and easy to change so you can try on clothes."

"I'm touched" she said sleepily. "You have assassins hunting you like some kind of high-priced game and you are worried about my wardrobe."

"Don't thank me just yet, we ain't exactly buyin' lingerie and evening gowns."

She twisted her delicate lips into a mock pout.

"You have about thirty minutes before we make the beach house." He patted her fanny playfully and strolled out of the room.

The Florida sun was stair stepping its way down through fluffy cumulus clouds on the powder blue western horizon when Hope ambled onto the aft deck. It seemed a lifetime since she'd seen the beach house perched ominously atop the sandy bluff. She joined James in the midafternoon heat on the dock quite content to be back on dry land.

He led her up the external stairs to the master bedroom. Once there he promptly stacked three heavy aluminum attaché cases by the door. Once there he carried a black nylon sports bag from the closet out to the living room balcony and tossed it over. When he returned he collected a second nylon bag and began loading guns and ammo into it. After the bag was packed he carried the attaché cases one by one to the 'Griffin'. Once that was done he slipped a .357 into a pancake holster and clipped it to his waistband in the small of his back. Collecting the remaining canvas bag he led Hope down the stairs where he picked up the bag tossed down minutes before and led her to the garage where he packed the bags into the Corvette.

"James." Hope said "can I ask a question without pissing you off?"

"Depends on the question..."

"Where are we going?" She said after a pause.

"To see a friend of mine."

"You always take that many guns to see a friend?"

"You'll understand when we get there." He shot her a quick smile. "For the record I doubt I'll have to kill him."

Chapter 19

The traffic was sparse on Interstate 4 between Cocoa Beach and Orlando so the miles passed quickly. James, Hope thought, seemed content to listen to Iron Maiden sing about a laughing profit and madness. She on the other hand fretted over the dilemma of her situation; there were enough small arms in the car to seize a town and she had no doubt he intended to use them. From a duty standpoint she had an obligation to stop him, had taken an Oath against the likes of Griffin James. But she was caught in a turmoil of emotion. He had, after all, saved her life once for sure and probably twice if she took into consideration the assault at the cove. Not to mention the fact that for all his illicit activity and his shortcomings he had touched an inner place in her that she had not realized existed. At the thought of the exotic pleasure she'd experienced at his hands, she entwined her fingers in his.

They turned onto a two lane highway on the outskirts of Orlando a few minutes later they pulled up in front of a plain block building with oxidized chipped white paint with Army Surplus scrolled over the buildings only door.

James unzipped one of the nylon tote bags and to Hope's surprise it was stuffed full of rubber-banded bundles of one hundred dollar bills.

"What's that for?" She asked, failing to hide her shock.

"To buy stuff," he said, as he grabbed three of the bundles and a Smith & Wesson .38 Special which he promptly put in a small paper sack.

James locked the car, set the alarm, and with Hope in tow entered the warehouse style surplus store. Inside there was every type of legal military surplus one could imagine stacked floor to ceiling. Remnants of American wars.

At the sight of them a pudgy, balding, middle-aged man with a flat top haircut came out from behind the sales counter.

"James," the flat top man offered a hand. "How the hell are you doing?"

"We alone?" James mumbled in response.

"Except her." Boss pointed a stubby finger at Hope, nearly touching her breast.

"She's with me" James grumbled pushing Boss's hand away. "And it ain't polite to point."

"We're alone," Boss answered chuckling, his beady eyes sizing up Hope like a lobster on display at a restaurant. "What'cha need?"

"Ten fragmentation grenades, three 9mm silencers and a sawed-off 12gauge. Pull the plug and put six white phosphorous rounds in it." James rattled off the list like he was requesting nuts and bolts from a hardware store clerk.

"Got the money," Boss asked rubbing his meaty hands together.

James pulled the .38 from the bag and tucked it down the front of his pants. Then he handed the sack to Boss. "Thirty G's in the bag. I need a few accessories, but that should cover it."

Boss smiled like a tomcat sitting next to an empty fishbowl. He pushed past them, locked the door and turned the sign around to indicate *closed*.

James and Hope worked their way through the mountains of the forest green canvas tents and trenching tool racks to the corner of the building. From a plywood display James selected a pair of camouflage shorts and a matching tank top.

"Take your clothes off," he said offhandedly.

She considered protesting, but the look in his eye was serious and impatient. She felt a self-conscious blush warm her cheeks and reminded herself how silly her embarrassment was. Obediently she stripped down to her panties and bra. A tingle ran through her when she saw the carnal desire in his eyes as they drifted over her body. He handed her the clothing, but caught her wrist before she had a chance to start dressing. Pulling her tight against him, he grabbed a fistful of her hair, tilted back her head and kissed her hard on the mouth. Then just as urgently he pulled away.

"Put those on," he said, pointing at the clothing he'd handed her. "Before Boss comes back. He's a pervert."

Hope's chest rose and fell breathlessly stunned by the brute force of his impulsiveness. She watched him disappear around a corner shelf before she slid into the shorts and shirt. She was impressed at the fit and his perceptiveness of her size.

He returned with an arm load of articles that he dropped at her bare feet. He helped her slip on a pair of dyed black knee-high leather moccasin boots. Next she wiggled into a set of jungle fatigues and a pair of calf high paratrooper boots.

"You make a sexy soldier girl," he said as he grabbed the front of her long-sleeved fatigue shirt and drew her to him. "You wanted to stay with me – I hope you're ready for what comes next."

The look in his eyes terrified her but she steeled her resolve. She knew it was far too late to turn back now. "And what comes next?"

"You'll see. Put your other clothes back on," he said. As she began to undress, his pale blue eyes traveled over her near nakedness.

On the way back to the front of the store he picked up three cans of Deep Woods Off bug repellent and two army green nylon bandolier belts. As they passed the counter, Boss, who was smiling like a jackass eating briars, handed James a forest green duffel bag. James nodded his thanks as he and Hope walked into the heat of the mid-day.

When they were back on the highway Hope considered for the first time how easily James had just purchased white phosphorous rounds, hand-grenades and silencers. This is crazy she thought, but hell, at least she wasn't ATF.

When they returned to the beach house James wasted no time loading the rest of their supplies onto the *Griffin* and by early evening they were once again out at sea. As James piloted the vessel, Hope was content to ponder her thoughts. At first she tried to convince herself that she hadn't lost control of her situation or switched loyalties, but the undeniable events that had transpired in the past few weeks left her to wonder who the bad guys were. James, without question, was a drug dealer, an addict, and a stone cold killer, but he held fast to his twisted sense of morals. On the other hand she had to question where the loyalties of the people on her own team lay. She wasn't certain that Hawthorn was dirty, but he had sent her undercover to work on Jason Tess. Then... the fact that she had notified him of her whereabouts on the night before the attack at the cove. It all seemed like more than just coincidence. Twice she escaped certain death narrowly, and only thanks to Griffin James.

"Penny for your thoughts" he said, as though he'd already been reading her mind.

"Just wondering we're we're headed," she lied.

"Probably Freeport to refuel tomorrow, but at the moment we're only about twenty miles off the coast and just north of West Palm Beach. We'll be dropping anchor for the night in a little while. I don't want to get to Freeport before early afternoon tomorrow"

"Freeport?" She asked.

"Yeah, it's on an island 'bout fifty or sixty miles off the mainland almost due east from West Palm. I want to avoid the mainland as much as possible," he said matter-of-factly. "And we have some time to kill anyway."

True to his word, a few minutes later he brought the vessel to a halt and lowered the anchor. Hope hadn't really known what to expect when they stopped for the night, yet she found herself anticipating his touch. While he buttoned down the hatches and readied the vessel for a night at sea, she found herself in the master suite freshening up and dressing as seductively as her meager wardrobe allowed. Bra-less under a nearly sheer top with the most revealing panties she had with her, she slipped under the satin sheets covering the mammoth bed and waited wantonly for him.

When he entered the room her desire broke and her own uninhibitedness shocked her. Almost before he reached their bed she was crawling all over his enticing body. Never had she been so brash, but her desire didn't allow for shame or embarrassment. She took what he offered and gave all she was to him, anyway he chose to take her, and take her he did with a vigor unlike she'd ever experienced. He again proved to be a tireless lover and instinctively he knew exactly when and where to touch her. He took her until she had nothing left to give. Realizing her exhaustion, he cradled her in his arms and together they found peace in the sanctuary of deep sleep.

Again she woke alone on the enormous bed for a second day her lithe body was sore, a remnant of their sexual experience, but guilt was creeping its way into her mind. She knew she had crossed the line, but how could she take it back now? What was worse, she wasn't sure she wanted to. What was she thinking? Slipping from the comfort of the satin sheets she moved to the bathroom. Maybe a hot shower would help her regain her focus.

Standing under the steamy spray her resolve began to return as the hot water chased away the lingering sensation of his caresses. By the time she toweled off and dressed, her cop instincts had returned, at least to some degree. It was that instinct that reminded her of the attaché cases. Quickly she began to search the room and was rewarded almost immediately. She found the cases stacked in the chest at the foot of the bed. She held her breath as she tried the latches of the top attaché case. The metallic click was loud in the stillness as the latches sprung open. She paused unsure if she dare open the case. But then it was her job, she thought, taking a deep breath she flung back the lid and gasp. "Oh my God!" She said aloud.

"Well that's one way to put it" James said from the door.

Startled she spun to face him. "Oh James I-I can explain" she stammered. Something changed in his eyes, and fear wracked through her body.

"I've got a better idea" he stated flatly "I'll explain you're looking at about eight hundred Gold Eagles and at market price that's just over seven hundred thousand in pure untraceable gold. Not to mention the other two cases hold about the same." He grabbed her by the wrist and pushed her back on the bed.

Too terrified to move she watched him storm to the closet and with great effort slung a canvas bag on the bed next to her. "That is around two and a half million in good ole' fashion American hundreds. Now is there anything else you'd like to know?"

Hope shook her head still in a state of terror.

"Good because I don't like people poking around in my personal business!"

After he left in a huff, she lay on the bed and cried. She cried because she was scared and because she had betrayed her oath, but also she cried because she could no longer deny the fact that she loved him. Her feelings were in complete contrast to everything she had ever believed in, and try as she might she could find no way out of her situation. Confusion turned to hate and hate she did. She hated her job, her boss, and most of all she hated the way she loved him. That thought brought a new wave of tears and she cried until exhaustion claimed her body and she drifted off into fitful sleep.

A loud bang rippled through the *Griffin's* hull jarring Hope from a tormented dream. Lying on the bed trying to orient herself to her surrounding the sound came again. Groggily she stumbled from the room and up to the main deck where the twilight of early evening shimmered its fading light on the distant horizon. Standing at the main cabins external door Hope watched as James and a man she'd never seen loaded plastic drums onto the deck of the *Griffin*. When they had amassed ten drums on the deck, James handed the stranger a wad of money and with a grunt the man tossed the mooring line to James and shoved the *Griffin* away from the dock. James glanced her way as he strode the external stairs to the main bridge, but he gave no smile, nor did he falter in his stride. Moments later the *Griffin's* engines fired and the vessel lurched forward and headed out to sea.

This cold demeanor instantly brought Hope's earlier torment to the forefront of her troubled heart. She was straddling the fence and very close to being caught in the middle of two different worlds. However, the emptiness she felt at his cold indifference left a hollowness in her that she never would have believed existed. After a moment's consideration she climbed the stairs to the bridge.

"Can we talk, James?" She asked timidly.

"'bout what?" He said coldly.

"This morning. I-I'm sorry." She faltered on the edge of emotions.

"Come here" he extended his hand to her. When she was seated in his lap he continued "Hope I'm twice as smart as you think and I'm way out on a limb where you're concerned. I hope I'm not wrong about you." He reached up and turned her head so he could look into her emerald eyes. "Don't disappoint me Hope"

"I won't." She whispered snuggling into his embrace.

Chapter 20

"Wake up, Hope." He whispered urging her from her nap on his lap.

"Where are we?" She looked groggily through the vast windows of the bridge. The night was inky black and only the instrument panels provided light in the cabin, it was no more than a warm glow.

"We just entered the Florida Straits. We'd be in the Gulf in a few hours, but I need a pick-me-up and I can't do that with you on my lap."

"A pick-me-up? What's that?"

"Look over there in the third drawer." He pointed "give me the black bag right on top."

Hope retrieved the bag reluctantly. "I hope that's not what I think it is." She said handing him the bag.

He unzipped the bag and removed a syringe ignoring her words.

"I'm not watching this," she said in disgust. "I can't believe you're a junkie!" Hope stormed off the bridge, by the time she cleared the stairs James had pushed the needle home and emptied the syringe into his vein.

James, high now, his mind working overtime, hardly knew the passage of time. Only the fuel gauge enabled him to realize it had been several hours. Shutting down the engines he climbed down to the deck and began pumping fuel from the barrels on the deck into the *Griffin's* tanks. When he'd emptied the last plastic drum he threw the empty barrels over the side and turned toward the main cabin.

There she stood backlit by the low lights of the cabin, he couldn't see her face, but her defiant stance spoke volumes. He strolled to where she stood and as she started to speak he placed a finger to her lips. "I don't want to talk about it, please?" Without another word he stepped past her and climbed the interior stairs to the bridge.

Day was breaking when James found a small island near Cape Sable where they could drop anchor. He was tired; the effects of the meth had long passed. He climbed to the lower deck, but didn't see Hope when he entered the Master suite. Too tired to argue he showered, shaved and crawled into bed, asleep almost before his head hit the pillow. He slept like the dead.

Night was falling and the Master Stateroom was cast in eerie shadows when James opened his eyes. Slowly his eyes searched the shadows as he tried to shake his mind clear of the groggy effect of the much needed, dead-like sleep. The wake of her stare startled him and his eyes shifted quickly to the far corner of the room where her silhouette was just visible in the waning light. Her astute eyes gleamed back at him out of the shadows and conveyed Hope's still smoldering anger.

"Goddamn," he said in defense of her penetrating gaze. "Why don't you just kill me and get it over with?"

"Why would I do that?" She shot back, her voice boiling with temper. "When all I have to do is leave you to your own device and you'll kill yourself."

"Look" he said in a way of explanation. "What did you expect? I'm no saint, never claimed to be and you of all people know that. But if I shattered some illusions you had of who and what I am then I'm all apology."

"You don't get it, do you James?" Hopes earlier anger fading in her tone. "I refuse to sit around and watch you destroy yourself."

"So what are you saying? You want out? Well, it's too late for that, at least until we get where we're going."

"I'm your prisoner now?" She asked in contempt.

"No," he said calmly. "But we're together until we reach our destination, then if you want out you're free to go. However, I think you'll find that my actions are as much for you as for my own interest."

"What's that supposed to mean?"

"It means that in the end the truth always comes out and although I don't buy into that the *truth will set you free* crap I do believe the truth has a way bringing about change." When he finished speaking he let the silence stand in the face of her questioning stare.

Her questioning stare, she knew, was poor cover for the torment raging in her thoughts. Could he know? How? If he did know why not run? It was that thought that broke the silence between them "why not run?" Her words were just above a whisper.

He pondered her words for a while when his answer came his emotion was clear in his voice. "I just recently learned that the past will haunt you until you deal with the demons of yesterday. With that in mind I feel it best to confront my demons as they come. Besides the fact I ain't much on running."

Hope studied him in the darkness as he eased from the bed and slid on a pair of shorts. Her earlier anger forgotten, lost in the depth of his words. He was young and wise, and foolish at the same time, but he inspired loyalty and love. For all his faults she knew she would follow him to Hell and at least for now her secret was safe.

Her secret? God what was she thinking! She was duty-bound to bring them down, not crash and burn with them.

"I've got work to do." The touch of his hand shook her from her troubled thoughts. "Want to help?"

"Do what?" She asked, concentrating more on his fingers in her hair than his words.

"I'm gonna hide my gold on this island just in case things go bad."

Go bad? She thought, as he took her hand and led her to the main deck. *Could it get any worse?* She knew better than to ask.

On the main deck James carried the attaché cases of gold outside and placed them on the dive platform at the stern of the boat. Then he opened a storage chest and removed a shovel and a large coil of rope. That done he went back inside and retrieved a large plastic cooler. After tying the cooler to one of the attaché case, he tied one end of the rope to the case and the other end around his waist. With a shovel in one hand, he climbed from the dive platform.

"What do I do?" Hope asked, once he was in the water.

"Feed the line as I swim. When you run out of line push the cooler and the case into the water. The cooler will float and keep the case from sinking" with that he started swimming for the beach.

Hope fed the line as James had instructed her to do. When she came to the last coil of rope she pushed the heavy case and cooler into the rolling waves with a splash. She could no longer see James so she watched the white of the cooler lid slowly being pulled through the inky black water until it too disappeared in the darkness. Time seemed to march at a snail's pace and she continued to worry that something had happened to him. Although she had known him for about a year and really known him just the past few months, it seemed a lifetime. But, she couldn't help wonder how it was going to end. What if James found out who she really was? How could they ever be together? Could she walk away from her life and become a part of his? Their situation appeared hopeless.

The splashing sound of swimming brought her from her dreadful thoughts. He was safe and at least for the moment they were together.

"Miss me?" He asked around a crooked smile as he climbed onto the dive platform.

In answer she embraced him. The chill of the salty water on his skin soaking through her flimsy T-shirt combined with his touch sent goose-bumps through her lithe body. In his arm she felt safe and her troubles seemed world's away, part of some other life.

"Come on baby." James said, stepping out of her embrace. "I have two more trips to make." She watched as he pulled in the rope still attached to the cooler and for the first time in days she thought about the gunshot wound on his left arm. "How's your arm?" She asked knowing it must hurt.

"All right," he mumbled, dragging the cooler onto the platform. With practiced efficiency, he secured the next case to the cooler, brushed a kiss on her cheek and dove back into the water.

Again Hope fed the line and watched the white cooler lid disappear, but this time the weight was much shorter and the torment of her earlier thoughts had no time to return before James was back on the boat and securing the last case. As she fed the line and shoved the case in the water a powerful urge to be with him came over her. She quickly stripped to her panties and bra and dove into the chilly water. When she reached the beach James was shoveling sand into a large hole. He didn't appear surprised to see her when he glanced up from his task, but for a moment she felt naked and embarrassed under his gaze. A shiver ran through her as a breeze danced over her bare wet skin and she crossed her arm over her chest against the chill.

Once the hole was covered James placed the rope in the cooler and tossed the cooler and the shovel in the palmettos. Then like the wind he was on her, his touch dancing on her skin. When she could wait no longer she had him down on the sand, straddling him, with their eyes locked in passion she lowered herself, joining their bodies...

At daybreak when she opened her eyes she was looking directly at his eyes. She had no way of knowing how long he'd been awake or even if he had slept. All she could remember was collapsing on him in exhausted bliss and drifting off to sleep tangled in his embrace. Searching his eyes she found a change in his icy stare, a softness that she'd never seen before and she instinctively knew that she had somehow broken through to his ironclad heart. Gently his hands traced her body rekindling the fire of the night, but unlike the urgent, thrashing, uninhibited sex they'd had in the small hours of the morning this time he made slow sweet love to her.

~ ~ ~

Two days later they motored under the Sunshine Skyway Bridge and into Tampa Bay. As they passed under the magnificent structure James punched David's number into his cell phone.

"Yeah," David answered on the second ring.

"It's me. Dave. Are you ready?" James listened in silence for a few minutes and hung up.

"James," Hope said in a small voice, "are you sure you want to go through with this?"

James pondered her question and his answer before he spoke. "I don't want to do this, I have to. I thought explained that before."

"You did, but... I just thought you might change your mind."

James reached over and took Hope's hand. "The next few days will change our lives forever."

She gave him a questioning glance, but his words gave her a cold chill. "What is that supposed to mean?"

"You'll see," was all he said.

A few minutes later they eased up an inlet and glided smoothly up to a dock behind a mammoth house. James secured the *Griffin* to the dock and collected the two canvas bags he'd loaded in Cocoa Beach. With Hope in tow, they walked around the house. When they reach the driveway she was surprised to see his Corvette parked there. James tossed the bags in the back of the Vette and climbed behind the wheel.

"Where we going?" Hope asked, sliding in beside him.

"Pinecrest," he answered flatly as he backed the Corvette into the street and gunned the engine.

[157]

Thirty minutes later they nosed up to a ramshackle red barn with a tin roof that set behind an ancient house with clapboard siding. The grass was in dire need of mowing and the hedges had taken on the look of a young forest. The place looked as though it had been abandoned in the middle of some long-ago night.

"Who lives here?" Hope asked, her distaste plain in her sarcastic tone.

"I grew up here," he answered in a pride-laden voice as he climbed from the Vette.

She'd never considered his past. The James she knew drove a flashy car, lived in a mansion on the beach and spent money like he owned the printing presses. Humble beginnings just didn't fit into his persona. He exuded the knowledge and presence one associates with a silver spoon.

She watched him fling back the well-worn barn doors and fade into the dark interior. When he reappeared he was pushing a flat black four-wheeler equipped with racks and flotation tires.

"Can you operate one of these? He asked when she got out of the car.

"Sure."

He disappeared in the barn's inner darkness again returning with the first four-wheeler's twin brother. He seemed preoccupied with the task of unloading the Corvette and packing supplies on the four-wheelers. She was astonished at the way he wasted no movement, methodically he strapped the gear on the machines right down to a shotgun he placed in the handle bar rack. But for the first time he was making her nervous and with the passing of each minute he was becoming more distant somehow. She flirted with the idea of telling him she changed her mind about going with him, but when she looked around, the only house in sight was the one James grew up in. Butterflies fluttered in her stomach as she thought of his statement at the surplus store. Next we see where your heart is that. What did he mean? Was he losing his senses? Was she really going into the woods with him? And him, armed to the teeth!

The sound of a four-wheeler engine tore her from her thoughts. She hadn't even realized that he'd put the Corvette into the barn and closed the doors. Except for the trails where the tires had bent over the tall blades of grass you couldn't tell anyone had been here.

"Follow me." He ordered, climbing on the idling four-wheeler.

She was aware of his piercing eyes on her and she also knew it was now or never. She scanned the surrounding area again, deciding she had no other choice, and got on the four-wheeler.

She followed in his tire tracks around the barn, across a field and down into a creek bed that had no more than six inches of water trickling through it. The banks of the creek loomed over them like weed-covered castle walls with live oak trees for torrents. The going was rough. The four-wheeler, with its considerable payload, jolted and jerked under her as she kept pace with him twisting and turning with the flow of the creek. After what she estimated to be an hour into the journey they came to a place where the stream emptied into a small shallow river. Without hesitation James plunged into the river on his four-wheeler and she followed.

On the far side of the river they picked up a trail that had obviously been made by many years of passage. The trails snaked through the trees along the river, dipping in and out of the washes. It was at the top of one of these washes were James finally stopped.

Hope hopped off the four-wheeler anxious to stretch her cramping legs. She hadn't been able to see his face as they rode, but now what she saw terrified her. His mannerism had completely changed. His eyes were hollow and cold, his face was devoid of all emotion as he approached her. Wordlessly he un-strapped a black nylon sports bag from the four-wheeler Hope had been riding. Unceremoniously, he stripped off his T-shirt, soft side leather boots, and Levi's jeans. From inside the bag he produced a can of Deep Woods Off and began to spray himself down with the oily bug repellent.

After completely covering his skin, hair, and boxers he began to redress in camouflage clothing from the bag. Hope watched him put on a camouflage tank top and shorts, moccasin boots of black leather, fatigues and black paratrooper boots.

"Strip down" he said when he finished dressing.

"I'm okay," she stammered. "The bugs haven't been biting me."

"Of course they haven't but we're not in the swamps yet and it's not dark. When we get down in the swamps and the sun goes down the goddamn mosquitoes will suck you dry," he cracked a smile. "Now quit being shy and strip."

Reluctantly Hope undressed, still unsettled by the difference in him. Maybe, she thought, it was the fact that he was on his way to murder someone and it was weighing heavy on his mind, or maybe he knew they were in grave danger, but it just didn't seem like the James she'd come to know. He never worried about anything and confidence was definitely not a problem.

When she had taken off everything but her bra and panties he sprayed down the front of her body. Then he turned her away from him and sprayed down her backside. When he finished he tossed the can aside, wrapped his arms around her waist and nuzzled his face into her hair. She was relieved by his affection and began to relax in his embrace as she remembered the pleasures they'd shared.

"Agent Brooks" he whispered in her ear. "I think we need to have a talk."

Hopes breath froze in her chest and her heart doubled its rhythm. Primal fear raged through her and her mind reeled with the hopelessness of her situation. She considered denying it, but didn't dare chance angering him. "How'd you find out?"

"I had you followed the night I dropped you off at the hospital." He felt her tense. "I knew then that you were a cop but it took a couple days to find out you work for the DEA. To tell you the truth I wasn't really concerned until you showed up in Cocoa Beach."

She closed her eyes as he slid his hands down and grabbed her wrist. "So what happens now?"

"I already told you. We find out where your heart is." He paused as if considering his thoughts very carefully, when he spoke his voice was flat. "The way I see it you have two choices; you're with me or against me."

She could feel her heart hammering in her chest and knew he could too. "What happens if I'm against you?" She dared the question.

"Then I disable your four-wheeler, give you a 9 mm and you're free to go. You see, I know these woods. It's ten miles in any direction to the nearest road. It's rough country to hike during the day and near impossible to hike at night. It'll be dark soon, but I'll give you a gun. Lots of pit vipers and wild hogs around here." He dropped his right hand and began to stroke her hip.

God, she hated the fact that he knew just where to touch her. Why couldn't he be a working stiff? She leaned into him and asked the question she knew she shouldn't. "What if I'm with you?"

"I came back here for a reason and I intend to carry out my plan. Then I'm leaving the country. You know I have two and a half million in cash on my four-wheeler that I brought just in case I can't make it back to the *Griffin*. However, if I do make it back those three attaché cases have a total of twenty-four hundred Gold Eagles in them, plus I have over one million in cash at Paul's in the Bahamas. So the plan is to take the money and run. We'll find a place on a tropical island where we can lay on the beach and drink rum and Coke." He bit her neck playfully, "And do whatever else comes to mind."

Damn, she wished he'd quit touching her. She was having difficulty thinking clearly. She didn't care about the money, but she knew she could live a lifetime, ten lifetimes, and never find another Griffin James. He had effortlessly reached the places inside her that no man had ever come close to. She had to do something before she lost her nerve or came to her senses.

"Take your time," he whispered as he brushed a kiss across her cheek and strolled to the river's bank.

She looked at his profile for a moment and then whispered "I choose you James."

He cocked his head squinting his eyes in disbelief. "You realize what you're saying?"

She nodded.

"Dante isn't stupid, Hope. He'll be waiting for me to make my move. So make no mistake I may never see the sun come up in the morning and if you go with me you may not see the sun rise either." His voice was calm, almost chilling and deadly serious.

"Then why not just forget Dante and leave?"

"Because Dante tricked me into killing Warren Allison and I'll have to live with the fact that I killed a man that didn't deserve to die for the rest of my life. I can't take back what I did, but I can damn sure avenge Warren's death." He turned his head in shame and drew a deep breath. "I don't expect you to understand the fucked-up morbid principles I live by, but understand that I live in a world where calling in the cops is not an option, so we enact our own form of justice. I'm not saying I'm right, far from it, but tonight we let God decide who is right or wrong, and if I live through the night then it must mean I'm right. One way or the other this is my last fight. I win – I'm gone, if I don't..." He let the words trail off.

"Your last fight?" She repeated his words. "Then let's be sure to win."

"I love your spirit." He shot her a wicked smile. "Get dressed, but leave your jump boots off so I can show you something."

Her decision was made; she wouldn't question him. He lived in a crazy sub-culture; a lawless world and he was still alive, a testament to his ability to prevail. She dressed and when she stood on her moccasin covered feet in front of him he tossed a couple twigs on the ground.

"Step on one of them" he pointed to the twigs.

She stepped down hard and the twig snapped surprisingly loud.

"That sound could get us killed" he said matter-of-factly. "Now step on the other one real slow until you feel it with your foot then stop."

Hope followed his instruction "okay" she nodded her understanding. "So that's what these are for... I was wondering."

"That's one reason we're wearing them. Just remember slow soft steps. It will be pitch-black so they won't be able to see us and as long as they don't hear us, they won't know we're there."

"You said, that was one reason. What's the other reason where wearing moccasins?" She asked.

"You don't really want to know the answer to that question," he said clenching his jaw muscles. "Put your jump boots on. It's getting late and Hell's Bath is a few miles from here."

"Hell's Bath? What a name for a place." She said.

Chapter 21

James adjusted the 9 mm shoulder holster securing it to Hope's slender frame. He slid two fully loaded 16 round magazines in the spare clip pockets of the holsters right ribs strap and plugged in the headset into the radio transmitter fitted into the holsters crossed back strap.

"Can you hear me?" He whispered into the mouthpiece of his own headset.

"Loud and clear," she answered with a giggle. She felt giddy like a kid in a paintball arena.

He walked over to one of the four-wheelers and returned with a Glock 9 mm. "I trust you've used one of these," he said, screwing the silencer on the end of the weapons barrel.

His voice crackled through the earpiece of the headset making him seem distant. Even though he was no more than an arm's reach away the effect was disorienting. "Never with the silencer on it. Jesus, James that thing will get you an automatic twenty years in a federal penitentiary."

He laughed. "Once the killing starts what difference does it make how many other laws we break? They can give me ten thousand years, but I can only do about fifty of them."

He handed her the silenced 9 mm. "Safety's on and there's one in the pipe. The weapon has been modified. When you empty the magazine it will lock open, and the clip will automatically fallout. When you shove the new magazine in, the slide will automatically close and in the process will push the loaded clips first round into the chamber."

"Where the hell do you get this stuff?" She asked indicating the weapon, radio, and accessories.

"I'd love to tell you, but I can't. You're a cop." He chuckled at the jest.

She threw him a hard look that was barely discernible in the impending darkness.

He effortlessly picked her up and set her on the black ATV. When he turned on the ignition two toggle switches in the neck of the handlebars lit up. "The blue switch," he explained. "Is for the headlight and the red one is for the taillight. No one's following you so leave your tail light off and if I tell you to, kill your headlight immediately."

She nodded her head in understanding.

He pushed the flexible mouthpiece away from his face and leaned close to her. "Listen, if something happens, don't hesitate – shoot first and ask questions later."

Again, she nodded her understanding.

He first moved to mouthpiece and kissed her full on the lips, passionately hard. "Stay close to me, listen to what I say and will be just fine. I know these woods better than anyone alive and no one can outsmart me here." James got on the other ATV, took a quick glance over his shoulder at Hope, and pulled away.

Hope pondered her decision as she followed James down the winding muddy, rut filled woodland tract. How could she ever explain this to her family? Hell, would she ever be afforded the opportunity? Sorry Mom and Dad – I fell for a dope dealer and I'm never coming home. She played the scene over in her mind, again and again. It was wrong she knew, but it was her life and she couldn't deny the exhilaration he inspired in her, or the magic of his touch. Let the devil have tomorrow she resolved; what good was living if you didn't enjoy life?

The trail, now walled on either side by saw-grass too tall to see over, was mucky and switched back to and fro until it was impossible to discern any form of direction. Here and there a side branch would break off the path and twice they'd taken a short trail. Hope noticed that James never hesitated about a turn making it plain to see that he knew exactly where he was. When at last he pulled into a washed out crevice and stopped she figured it had taken them more than two hours travel time from the river to the crevice.

"We're leaving the four-wheelers here."

His metallic voice startled her when it echoed in the earpiece.

"Just sit tight while I grab the gear and we'll be on our way."

Moments later he materialized in the blackness next to her with a heavy satchel slung over his shoulder and a shotgun in each hand.

"It's a semi-automatic," he droned. "Twelve round drum, fully loaded with slugs and it kicks like a mule." He handed her the weapon. "Safety's on. The switch is at the front of the trigger guard."

"I've got the 9 mm, do I really need this?" She held the shotgun up.

"If we spook a wild hog and he charges you, I wouldn't suggest shooting it with a 9 mm because it will probably get you before you can kill it with a pistol." He pointed at the shotgun. "Now that will flip your average hog." He stroked her cheek with his thumb. "Stay close."

He helped her climb out of the crevice up to the meadow it cut through. Once in the meadow of knee-high grass and bramble bushes the half-moon reflected enough light to follow the narrow footpath that led to a distant stand of cypress trees. The night had been muggy and the air thick, but a stiff summer breeze rippled across the meadow.

They were only a few yards from the trees when Hope felt something strike her low in the right calf muscle, nearly toppling her to the ground. She drew a sharp breath to prepare her lungs for a startled scream, but when she saw the perpetrator of the blow, her scream froze in her throat.

James Heard Hope's sudden intake of air in his earpiece and spun around, bringing the shotgun up to a firing position, clicking off the weapon safety and pulled the slack out of the trigger.

He instantly saw the cause of her alarm and dropped the shotgun. In a flash he was on one knee next to her and by the moons light he caught the struggling cottonmouth water moccasin behind the head. Expertly he prodded the pit vipers jaw forcing its mouth open and untangled its fangs from the leg of Hope's fatigues. He thumbed opened the blade of his five inch lock blade and unceremoniously cut the cottonmouths head off and tossed its withering body into the swamp grass.

Without preamble he untied the right ankle drawstring of Hope's fatigue's and pushed the pants leg over her trembling knee. He loosened Hopes right moccasin and checked her leg for puncture marks. She was still shaking in horror when he found the spot where the snake had struck her. The attacked area was already red and puffy, the prelude to one hell of a bruise, but there were no puncture wounds. The leather moccasin had prevailed. He re-tied her boot and fatigues.

"You're okay" he whispered as he pulled her shivering body against him.

"W-was it p-poisonous?" She stuttered.

"Deadly poisonous. Welcome to Hell's Bath." He gave her a reassuring squeeze. "That stand of cypress trees is growing in a low land stagnant pool of runoff water. It's what we call a 'Bay Head' and considering this particular Bay Head is overrun by cottonmouths; we call it 'Hell's Bath'. Unfortunately we have to cross it. It's only fifty yards wide but it's three miles long, too far to walk around."

He picked up his discarded shotgun and put it in the satchel and took hers.

"Come on" he encouraged, offering her his free hand. "You got to trust me."

She laced her fingers in his and found courage in the contact. He, she thought, lived by his advice. He'd told her not to hesitate and when the time for action had risen he didn't falter, but rose to the occasion. She wondered what exactly it would take to rattle him, then immediately abandoned the thought deciding that by the time he lost his composure he'd probably be dead.

He pulled up short at an enormous cypress that lay half submerged in murky, foul-smelling water.

"Watch your step Hope. If you fall in the water your'e subject to get snake bit a hundred times." He squeezed her hand.

"I thought they couldn't bite underwater?"

"That's an old wives' tale." He answered. "They can damn sure bite underwater."

They were partway across the slime crusted log when he stopped and although she couldn't see the reason, she felt him kick, heard a thud and then heard a splash. He gave her hand another gentle squeeze and they continued. The land rose steeply where the log ended at the edge of a narrow meadow bathed in moonlight. They quickly crossed the open area of the field and walked into another stand of trees with a canopy so thick they were cast in complete darkness, but after a dozen yards James shined a penlight on a massive live oak tree with boards nailed to the trunk forming a makeshift ladder.

Hope followed James up the slat ladder to a rail-less platform eight-foot wide and ten foot long. "What now?" She asked as she lay down on her back, shoulder to shoulder with James.

"We wait for David and Wes." James checked his watch "we're forty-five minutes early."

"Where are we?" She questioned anxious to keep the conversation alive.

"About five hundred yards behind Dante's house," he said taking off his headgear. "You can wait here if you want to. It's safe."

She too, pulled off her headgear. "I want to stay with you James. I feel safe with you." She found his hand in the darkness. "What do you fear James? I mean," she stammered, "you always appear so calm and in control."

"Fear," he said distractedly. "Only hinders you when you allow it to. In my experience when you want to check a real man or you want to measure a man's grit, watch how he plays when he's dealt a shitty hand. Scared money folds a bad hand, but the confident man takes the gamble because he believes in his ability to overcome and endure."

She considered his words under the stifling hot and sticky blanket of darkness that shrouded them. For all his insane antics and his reckless disregard for the law she determined that he wasn't without morals or principles, but a throwback to a long forgotten way of life. Her mind conjured up a picture of him; a black leather lowboy pulled over his squinting eyes, jaw muscle clenched, bandanna knotted at his throat, an open rawhide vest partially covering his chest, denim boot-cut jeans over the dingoes with spurs jingling at the well-worn heels and a pearl-handled six gun slung low on his hip and tied down.

She giggled.

Then she watched the mental image of him amble out on the dusty main street of a ramshackle western town and square off against some nameless adversary. She held her breath as his fingers danced in the air above the pearl handles of his six-shooter. With blinding speed he drew, firing from the hip and sent three rapid shots over the dusty expanse and into the chest of the faceless man who had failed to clear leather.

Then with a backward spin he holstered his weapon and strolled toward the town's saloon tipping his hat to every swooning lady he passed along the way.

The touch of his hand snapped her back to the present century and the reality of his words reminded her of the chaos she had willfully embraced when she opted to switch sides.

"Someone's coming" his mouth was pressed to her ear his words barely audible. "Stay down and put your head gear back on." He kissed her cheek. "I'll be back."

With cunning stealth he blended into the inky blackness and was gone.

Hope strained to hear movement over the pounding of her heart, but detected nothing. James had disappeared without so much as a sound; she doubted she could have performed the same feat in the light of day never mind trying in the charcoal blackness. One thing was obvious, he was definitely a woodsman.

Crack! She heard the twig snapping out in the night. She was surprised how loud such a slight sound seemed in the deadly silent night. Someone isn't wearing their moccasins. She thought, with a smile, back to the lesson James had given her a few hours ago.

A boot scuffing the base of the tree sent a frigid chill along her spine. *Don't hesitate*, James words echoed in her mind sending her hand to the butt of the 9 mm strapped to her side. She drew the weapon and fingered off the safety pointing the barrel at the place where the ladder accessed the platform.

"Well Griffin James, if you measure a man by his confidence, how do you measure a woman?" She whispered the words to the night.

"I measure a woman by her loyalty and don't call me Griffin."

The sound of his voice reminded her she was wearing the headgear. She had not meant for him to hear her words and the heat of her sudden embarrassment spread through her, but before she had a chance to dwell on her shame, a hushed conversation cracked through the earpiece.

"Y'all are seven minutes late." James voice stated.

"Jesus Christ James, you ain't gotta sneak up on us!" David's startled voice.

"Y'all ready?" James' voice questioned.

"Yeah" David and Wes said in unison.

"Wait in the field, I'll get the gear." James's voice said again.

Minutes later, satchel over his shoulder, James led Hope by the hand into the moonlit meadow where they joined David and Wes.

James, anxious to enact his plan, outfitted his makeshift hit squad, starting with David to whom he gave headgear and transmitter, a silenced 9 mm with shoulder holster and extra clips. Next he gave Wes headgear and transmitter, a 12gauge semi-automatic with twelve round drum, a bandolier loaded with spare rounds, a clip on holstered .357 and three grenades.

Chapter 22

"Radio check." James announced. "You got me David?"

"Clear."

"Wes?"

"Clear."

"Hope?"

"Clear."

"Okay"

"Y'all listen to close. We work in two-man teams. Wes − Dave − y'all take the north side and the front of the house." James instructed. "Hope and I will take the back and the south. Just try to get a visual until we have a feel for what we're up against. If you have to use a weapon before we're in place use a silent one. Any questions?"

"Yeah" David chimed in. "How come you get the girl on your two-man team?"

Wes, who stood next to David laughed and looked at Hope who was standing next to James a few feet away and glaring at David.

"That's easy David." James shot back. "I get the girl because I'm smart enough not to get caught with my pants down. Now let's get going."

James collected Hope's hand and they faded into the shadows of the trees. Surefooted he led her through the darkness and underbrush.

She was amazed at the way he seemed to know precisely where he was going in spite of the pitch blackness. After several minutes they emerged from the trees at a shallow narrow stream, where they disposed of their jump boots and tucked their fatigues into their moccasins. They walked upstream in the water for what hope estimated to be three hundred yards before they stopped.

James pushed the flexible mouthpiece away from his face and pulled his lips to hopes right here. "If something happens and we get separated, you come back here and follow this creek downstream to the river and wait for me there." He hooked her hip and pulled her body against his. "Are you sure you want to be a part of this?"

She nodded her head vigorously. She wanted to tell him that she'd do anything for him, but didn't. No one had ever made her feel the way he did and she knew no one ever would again.

He kissed the top of her head, stepped back, adjusted his mouthpiece and drew the 9 mm from his shoulder with his free hand and motioned her to follow.

They moved slower now and occasionally Hope glimpsed a light through the trees. Almost like magic, a clearing appeared and at its center one hundred yards away sat a mansion she instinctively knew belonged to Dante Westhardt. The house and outbuildings were well lit, as were the two armed guards standing next to what appeared to be a bungalow style guesthouse. How James intended to dispose of the guards with a pistol, at what she guessed to be sixty yards she couldn't fathom, but one thing was sure – she was glad she wasn't one of the guards. Experience had revealed time and again James' uncanny knack to prevail.

"Jay, we're set." David's voice in the ear piece. "And there looks to be three guards between the fountain and front porch."

"Can you take them down, Dee?"

"Yeah, but we'll have to break cover more toward the back of the house so they can't see us move."

"I've got two back here that have a plain view of the sides Dee, so you'd better let me take them first."

"Copy Jay. Let me know when we're clear."

Hope glanced over the layout of the buildings and the landscape and again wondered how the hell James intended to cross sixty yards of manicured lawn cross hatched in floodlights. True to form James didn't keep her in suspense, before she realized, he'd moved. He was twenty yards away, shotgun slung over his back, and belly-crawling his way straight for the guards. She couldn't believe his lunacy and what's more, she couldn't believe that the guards hadn't seen them yet. Hell, she thought, he's in plain view; the son of a bitch is crazy. But the longer she watched, the more amazed she became with his ruse. He had covered two thirds of the distance when, with deliberate ease, he stretched his arms out, his hands cradling the silenced 9 mm and with what seemed no remorse, killed both men. She knew they were dead, she'd seen their heads jerk violently with the impact of his shots. First one then the other, a split-second later, crumpled to the ground.

Hope couldn't help but be impressed with his marksmanship – a headshot at sixty feet – but the harsh reality settled in quickly; a lot of men were going to die here tonight. She closed her eyes in silent prayer. God – I'm in love with a cold-blooded killer.

"Dee, your clear to move," James broke the silent airwaves. "You too Hope."

Hope covered the distance to the bungalow rapidly. When she reached James she tried not to look at the bodies that lay next to the building.

"Dee, let me know when you're in position." James said, motioning Hope to follow him.

They darted through the brilliant pools of amber light and took cover behind the fountain twenty yards away from the sliding glass door that was the rear entrance into the mammoth home. He holstered his 9 mm and took the shotgun Hope was carrying with his left hand. With his right hand he pulled the 9 mm Hope wore under her left arm and handed it to her. Silently, the mouth "Be ready," and glanced around the back yard searching for movement. When he was satisfied that they remained undetected he turned to face the glass door and leveled the shotgun at the door's center.

"Jay, we're set." David's voice was hushed, but dripping with the heat of the moment exhilaration.

"Wes," James instructed in a level, calm voice. "I want you to pull the pin on a grenade and let the spoon fly when I say *One*. I'm gonna count to seven, but when I get to three I want you to toss the grenade at their feet. It should go off when I get to seven. Let the dust settle and then cover the front. Hope and I are going in the back on seven. Copy?"

"Copy," came Wes's voice almost immediately.

Hope couldn't help but admire James' calm. Her heart thumped an impossible crescendo in her ears and the 9 mm shook in her trembling hands. He, on the other hand, held the semi-automatic shotgun stock still, the picture perfect model of composure.

"On my count," James started. "Ready, and one, two, three..."

Hope could picture the grenade soaring through the air. The confused faces as it bounced at the guard's feet. Confusion changing to alarm as the realization set in that it was already too late.

"Five... Six..."

Ba-Boom! The grenade and shotgun went off nearly simultaneously. The effect was numbing, the mansion shook and rumbled as glass shattered. James, who was poised for the charge, saw the whooshing blue flash and dove into Hope driving her into the fountain and crashing in on top of her.

The explosion that ensued bathed the fountain in a shower of flame and quaked the ground under them. In a mushroom effect wood, metal, and the glass launched into the sky only to be collected by gravity and dragged back to earth as a deadly rubble rain.

James pulled a dazed, confused, and nearly drowned, Hope out of the waist deep, debris littered, fountain and found that where moments ago a picturesque southern style mansion sat, there was only an unintelligible pile of scorched refuse smoldering in the dusty smoke-filled night.

Almost at once James heard the repetitive thumping of the helicopter's blades pounding the air and closing fast. He grabbed Hope, who was still disoriented, by the hand

and dashed for the cover of the trees, drawing the silenced 9 mm from its holster as he ran. He and Hope were twenty-five yards from the tree line when the radiant white spotlight bathed them in its brilliance. Without breaking stride or taking time to aim the Glock, James fired over his left shoulder in the general direction of the invading helicopter until the weapons slide locked back and the magazine dropped out of the handle.

The helicopter circled and began to return fire as they dove headlong into the underbrush and bramble. James, in one practiced motion, slammed a fresh clip into the 9 mm as the helicopters bullets ripped through the foliage, ricocheting wildly off the trees. He rolled onto his back and fired three quick shots up through the canopy at the blinding light as the helicopter raced past. Without waiting to see if his shots were effective James snatched Hope up by the arm and set out at a dead run. Bramble thorns tore at their legs and branches slapped them, stinging in the face, as they crashed through the woods.

The white spotlight sliced through the dense twisted branches of the pines and water oaks searching the undergrowth for a couple hundred yards off their right flank. Meanwhile in a tumbling tangle of caution-less flight James and Hope spilled over the steep briar congested creek bank and sprawled face-down in the ankle-deep water.

Hope's whole body throbbed in wracking spasms of searing pain and she was having problems discerning what had caused the horrendous explosion, but she had no illusions about the helicopter or the flag it flew under. She need not see the five-point star to know it belonged to the local Sheriff's office and James had opened fire on them.

Well, she thought, *in for a penny – in for a pound*. No sooner did the thought flicker through her mind, did James jerk her a roughly out of the water. Automatic gunfire tore a straight line of momentary circular holes through the water where her head had laid a millisecond before he'd hauled her to her feet.

The light swept up the stream and locked its illuminating beam around them. Hope froze in the horror of certain death as yet another barrage of small caliber missiles bore down on them. If Hope hadn't closed her eyes in resignation of their fate, she would have seen James square his shoulders, take aim and fire three successive 9 mm rounds into the powerful bulb of the searchlight, causing the helicopter to bank right defensively, abandoning the chase for the time being.

James peeled away his malfunctioning headgear and transmitter. Then he removed Hopes, also useless, equipment while he whispered soothing words of encouragement to her, but to no avail. Hope was despondently unresponsive in her state of terror-induced shock. James knew the Sheriff's office wouldn't give up easy. Therefore, to have any chance at escape it was imperative to keep moving or risk almost certain capture.

He scooped Hope up in the cradle of his arms and trudged into the woods. James considered his decisions as he walked and the weight sat heavy on his mind. David and Wes had no chance to survive the explosion — hell he and Hope were damn lucky to be alive — but the simple fact remained that David and Wes were dead because he'd underestimated Dante. Maybe it was too late for David and Wes, but he was still alive. The need to avenge them surged through him, but just as quickly the voice of reason chimed in and expressed the obvious: this was a trap and the person responsible for their deaths was out of his reach. Dante had to know they were coming and set a trap for them. *How stupid of me*, James thought. It was simple but effective trap. Just blow out the pilot lights and turn on the stove. Then one little spark and the house goes off like a Roman candle.

~ ~ ~

"Yeah," Mayhew answered the phone, his voice gruff with sleep.

"Mayhew?"

"Yeah Captain."

"Duty calls. Dante Westhardt's house blew up a few minutes ago and we've got bodies everywhere. I need you to get your ass out there and figure out what the fuck's going on."

"Okay Captain, I'm on my way," Mayhew said, fully awake now.

"Mayhew there's one more thing."

"What's that Capt?"

"A man and a woman shot up our helicopter," the Captain paused. "I think it was Griffin James and Agent Brooks. Hawthorn will meet you there and needless to say Brooks may have went rogue, so don't trust her until we can confirm her loyalty."

"Got it Capt." Mayhew scrambled out of bed.

Five minutes later Mayhew raced, lights flashing, through the streets of Brandon. But his thoughts flashed by ten times as fast as the houses that lined the tranquil streets.

Something was wrong, Griffin James teamed up with a rogue Brooks, at war with Dante Westhardt? Why? That was the million-dollar question. How many more people had to die before he figured this mess out?

Mayhew was so wrapped up in his thoughts that he nearly missed the drive to the Westhardt Ranch. When he finally made the turn, what he saw took his breath away. On the knoll where the sprawling ranch house once sat there was nothing but a pile of burning rubble.

He pulled to a stop between the army of squad cars and emergency vehicles parked haphazardly around the smoldering ashes. Hawthorn met him almost before his feet were on the ground.

"Mayhew, we've got one hell-of-a mess here." Hawthorn said, on approach.

"Give it to me," Mayhew said exasperated, shaking his head.

"We've got seven bodies for sure, two of which are David Jones and Edmund Westhardt. No ID on the other five, but two were shot in the head by the guesthouse." Hawthorne leveled his gaze at Mayhew. "Did your Captain tell you the rest?"

"A quick summary, but give me the long version."

"Apparently y'all had a helicopter in the area when the house blew up so they circled around this way. When they came over the trees they saw Griffin James and Agent Brooks running for the trees. According to them, James fired on them and they returned fire." Hawthorn paused to let his words sink in. "But James and Brooks made for the trees and escaped."

"Where does that put Brooks in your mind?" Mayhew asked.

"On the wrong side. She hasn't checked in, in a couple weeks. And although that happens from time to time in deep cover situations, I can come up with no reason for her to get involved in mass murder."

"Point taken." Mayhew said. "What now?"

"We search the woods and swamps until we find them and bring them in or take them down."

Mayhew laughed.

"What is it that you find so amusing detective?" Hawthorn asked in distaste.

"You'd need an army of canines and officers, and then you'd need a lot of luck to get Griffin James out of the swamps." Mayhew shook his head and wrinkled his brow. "James knows these woods better than anyone alive. He could spend months, maybe years, in these parts and never be seen."

"Well, what do we do? Wait around until they kill somebody else?"

Mayhew thought for a moment. "I have an idea. I might know someone who will help us, someone from James' past."

"Something I can do to help?" Hawthorn asked.

"No, I'll set up patrols and organize a search, but I doubt we'll get anything that way."

"I have a stake in this too." Hawthorn said. "I'd like to know your plans. I've got an agent out there and people to answer to. Plus, I have resources that far exceed the meager selection you have to choose from."

"Do what you want, but you're wasting your time and resources as you put it." Mayhew smiled. "But then what do I know. I've only known James in a professional capacity for ten or twelve years."

"Do It Your Way, Mayhew, keep me posted." Hawthorn said in a huff and stomped off...

Mayhew worked his way carefully around the scene, not that there was much left to see. The place looked as though it had been the subject of a missile attack and try as he may he couldn't make the pieces fit. He for one would never have guessed that James could be this violent and for the life of him couldn't imagine what Dante Westhardt could have done to set the young man off on this murderous path.

He approached a lab-tech collecting evidence. "Can you tell me any more than the obvious?" Mayhew asked.

"Not really. Seven dead, two by gunshot, weapons everywhere; they were all armed for war." The tech scratched his head. "Both sides were prepared to fight to the death, but the explosion killed more than the fight."

"What caused the blast?"

"Don't rightly know," the tech said. "But it was one hell-of-a blast. I don't know how anyone lived through it."

"Thanks," Mayhew said walking back toward his car. He couldn't help but wonder, as he walked, if James was that good or just getting lucky...

Chapter 23

Nearly five years he thought, since he'd been to this place. Time had not changed it much judging what he could see in the waning light. The pale gray light pushed its way through the high canopy of the cypress trees, into the lower foliage of ancient water oaks and spilled its rippling reflection on the water's surface.

The river, he knew, was in many ways like time and yet different. Like time, the river never stopped, always twisting and turning. Like time it could rush for a while, or just amble along, but it never stopped and no man controlled it. Where and when it started no one could say, like ways who could say where it's water went after they spilled into Tampa's bay.

To him the river never changed much. It's amber waters traveled the same path he remembered, the trees had grown lush, a bit taller and thicker over the past five years since he was last here. But things seem to be pretty much the way he'd left them all those years before. That alone was the difference between his river and Old Man Time.

Old Man Time changed things, scarred people. It had taken him over twenty years to understand that. People feared Time because they knew every second brought them one second closer to the end of their allotted time. That knowledge turned life chaotic for most, always in a rush, they never stopped to enjoy life. Too worried *Time* would bring the end before they were ready. So they wasted a lifetime preparing, never really discovering what it felt like to be truly alive. Why blame Time he thought? It was and always would be what you made of it.

What had he made of his time? He wondered. The question had haunted him for years, years of silence – wasted years. The torment of wasted years had brought him back to this place, the place of his youth. But why? To remember? To forget? He couldn't say which, maybe because he intended to do both.

He remembered the first time he'd seen this place. The tranquil beauty had touched him somehow, drawn him in. The water spilling over the natural barrier of sandstone boulders as it swept through an arch and created an alcove of lush, soft grass at the inside base of the crevice. The gentle rippling of water, the only sound in the silence. At once he had claimed the place his. What had he been then? Maybe eight? He couldn't quite remember.

He climbed down the steep slope of the crevice to the alcove. There in the dense soft grass he sat in the late afternoon sun. For hours he watched the water fall and slosh over the rocks. A persistent breeze followed the water surface like a path to the sea, the cool light breeze dancing on his skin. He watched stringy white clouds stretch across the sky until the laziness of the afternoon overwhelmed him. Curling into a fetal position, he had fallen asleep in this place, his place. It had been a dream.

The dream had frightened him at first. A great black boar stood atop the slope. It's tusk enormous ivory blades curling away from its snout. With its razor-sharp tusk, the great beast was peeling away at the rugged bark off an old ancient oak. After a time his fear turned to awe. Then the Boar turned to face him, holding him in the wake of its inky black stare, his heart fluttered but not in fear. He could sense the beast meant him no harm, quite the opposite. The Boar came to protect him – from what he wasn't sure. Finally the great beast turned back to face the forest and stood rigid like a sentry, guarding him in the night.

He woke up in the twilight of the evening, the dream vividly clear in his young mind as he climbed the slope. It was then that he saw the tree. He couldn't remember it being there a few hours before when he discovered this place. A chill ran the length of his spine as his eyes found the spot, about chest high, where the bark had been

[182]

stripped away in the perfect shape of a "J", the first initial in his name.

He'd had trouble with sleep that night; he tossed, turned and contemplated. What did it mean? Was it really a dream? He didn't know, but he knew he had to go back. When sleep finally came it was a fitful, dreamless sleep. He'd woken the morning tired and anxious skipped breakfast and came back to this place. When or where he'd come up with the idea he didn't know, but when he reached the tree he knew what he had to do. With his pocket knife he carved the letters 'AMES' down the center of the "J" marking the tree forever his.

A strange sensation engulfed him as he found the ancient oak in the shadows. Slowly, reverently, he approached the tree finding the marking right where he knew it would be. It was still chest high, that he was a man now. The tree had grown with him. The "J" still a deep gouge, the letters down the center more faint then he remembered. But then five years had passed. Hands trembling, he traced the letters with the tip of his finger feeling the old magic flow through him. This was his safe place, his secret place, the place he'd come to when he needed to be alone.

But he hadn't always come here alone he remembered, they had shared this place. At her memory he stumbled more than walked to the edge of the slope. He almost expected to see her wading in the shallow waters, the way he had found her the summer he turned fourteen. Like a dam breaking in his mind, the memories came flooding back. He'd been angry when he'd first seen her wading in the shallows. He had almost called out his rebuke at her violation, her trespass, but the words caught in his throat. He knew who she was – her name was Yvette. She was older than him by a couple of years. She lived a few hundred yards from him. She always had an aloofness that kept them from becoming anything more than neighbors.

Now wading naked before him in the shallows she didn't seem so distant.

He decided, after a quick study of her body, she was more woman than girl. Her body looked as though it had been sculpted from marble and dipped in bronze. At first he turned away, ashamed, feeling like a pervert spying on her from the cover of the trees. After a moment he'd convinced himself that she wasn't real, just his imagination playing tricks. He'd never seen her here before and he'd been coming here for years. Turning back he saw her again, but different this time, even more stunning than before. Her hair dark from being wet, falling over her shoulders, breasts young and pert yet full. Her hips prominent below a slim waist, a touch of pubic hair between long slender legs. Her face like an angel, strong jaw, narrow chin with a slight cleft, lips full, nose graceful and delicate. Her eyes green, ablaze, accusing, staring at him.

He felt the heat of embarrassment climb his neck and settle on his face. He wanted to turn and run, run as fast as his feet would carry him, but like a deer caught in headlights, he was frozen in place by her audacious emerald green eyes. He'd recovered quickly from his embarrassment when she screamed at him.

"What the fuck you doing? You fucking asshole!" Her voice echoed up at him as she flung an arm and hand over her breast, the other hand dropping between her legs to cover her pubic hair.

With a boldness he didn't feel he had stepped forward, surprising himself with the confidence in his voice. He answered her angry question. "I thought I was watching an angel with a familiar face, but I doubt any angel has a mouth so foul."

The contempt had left her voice as she pleadingly asked him to turn around so she could dress. He had refused her request knowing he had the upper hand. Anger had flashed in her eyes, but also something else. With steps of raw confidence she had walked to her clothes and

[184]

dressed as if he was no longer there. He had watched in awe at her boldness, and her beauty.

She had dressed and climbed the slope walking towards him. She asked if he had enjoyed the show? But before he could answer she had glanced at his crotch and said. "Obviously you did." Without another word she had brushed by him, her scent lingering.

His embarrassment returned. He had not even realized his own arousal, so caught-up in the moment as he was. Finally finding his voice he turned in her wake and called out to her. "Yvette, hey look... I'm sorry!" His words had stopped her, but defiantly she hadn't turned around to face him. Yet her stance implored him to continue. "Look, you're right. I'm a fuckin asshole, but I... I couldn't help it. You caught me off guard and I really do think you're beautiful. So what can I do? I'll do anything!"

Smiling, she turned her face to him. "Anything?" She repeated.

He nodded his consent as something mischievous moved in her eyes.

"Then drop your shorts." The challenge in her voice daring him to coward out.

His anger flashed, she didn't think he would. Well, he wasn't a coward. With a quick snatch he'd pulled down his shorts exposing his semi-hardness. Under her stare he felt the same awkwardness she must have felt moments before.

"Ok we're even." She had said. She turned and disappeared into the trees. Leaving him standing there with his shorts around his ankles.

After all these years the memory brought a crooked smile to his face. That had been the beginning, a few days later he had been napping, as he often did, in the lush grasses of the alcove. She had crept up to where he lay, kneeling to kiss his lips. Her soft moist lips on his had startled him out of his slumber. Their heads had blotted as he struggled to sit up. It had taken him a minute to comprehend the situation. A minute they'd spent collectively rubbing the spots where their heads had collided. She had laughed, a husky, infectious laugh, and her radiant smile seemed to eclipse the midday sun. He had joined her in her laughter shaking his head in pleased disbelief...

He stumbled more than walked down the slope to the place where too many years before they had shared their laughter and so much more. He had pulled her down on him and they had kissed more passionately. He hadn't been sure what to do, he had never kissed a girl before. Not like this. He was painfully aware of her breasts pressing against his chest. He had nervously slid his hands from her waist to the roundness of her buttocks, the fabric of her shorts doing little to hide the firmness. She didn't seem to mind his exploring hands, in fact at his touch she began to grind her pelvis against his hardness. Encouraged by her response, he had brought his hands back up her sides bringing her T-shirt with them.

The feeling of her skin under his hands felt electric, goose-bumps chasing his fingers up her sides. She had risen to allow him to pull her shirt off. His eyes fell to the cream-colored bra covering her breast. He'd fumbled with the clasp; she'd sat up straddling him and unfastened it. Letting her bra fall from her shoulders. He studied her breast as she lay the bra aside, her nipples stiff at the bud-like center of her areolae. She helped him with his shirt. He would never forget the way she felt when she laid back on his bare chest, the silky softness of her breast on his pecks, her hard nipples trapped between them.

They had kissed again harder, more urgent this time. Slowly he had run his fingers down her spine, over her ass and between her legs. He could feel the heat of her sex through her cotton panties, silky and moist. Those too, he pushed aside. He felt her wetness, liquid heat spilling between his fingers. He'd begun to explore her. She tensed at the intrusion of his finger, a moan escaping her lips.

Time became a blur. How they'd finished undressing he couldn't recall. He remembered her laying before him.

The grass bringing out the color in her eyes, framing her body in a sea of greenness. He had entered her slowly, awkward, new to the motion. He'd felt her tautness, her breath catching as he forced himself into her. It was over quickly that first time. She had bled, and cried too. He remembered. He'd held her close when they were finished. Wordlessly they had shared the silence. The warm summer sun watching them as they laying naked in the grass. He didn't know that day he loved her, didn't know he would always love her.

It had been her first time, his two. Together they had sacrificed their innocence to the gods of desire. Her blood had been spilled here, as the sacrificial offering that had consecrated this place. Their place. Some fifteen years earlier. The cool night air was cold on the wet trail that tears left as they rolled off his cheek. Standing now on what he still considered hallowed ground, he failed to understand the cruelty of fate.

After more than a year of meeting here with her, fate had abandoned their love. He would never forget that day. He had come as he always did to meet her, but this day was different than all the rest. He found her, tears streaming down her beautiful face. He had pulled her close, held her tight, and asked what was wrong. She'd been so emotional that it had been nearly an hour before she could tell him. Her words, like a savage beast, had ripped his heart out. His whole life may have been different had her parents not divorced forcing her and her mother to move in with her grandmother in South Florida. They talked of running away, decided against it, and somehow each knew it was over. They made love several times that day and their paths hadn't crossed again until he'd showed up at the Cocoa walk. Although he'd seen her many times since that night, the magic was gone, lost in the years of bad memories.

The sharp snap of a twig chased away his thoughts of the past and spurred him into survival mode. Like a breeze, he moved up the slope and blended into the trees. With his pistol in his hand he waited, listening to the approaching footfalls echoed in the night. He could see a flashlight slicing through the darkness and he moved to overtake the intruders from behind...

"Drop the flashlight and step in front of it both of you and if you try to turn around your dead!" James's voice was eerie, calm and carried a lethal tone.

"James, please don't."

Yvette's voice took him by surprise, but did little to shake his resolve. "Yvette, do what I asked you to do."

Obeying his command she stepped into the light of the flashlight as did detective Mayhew.

"What the fuck you doing here Mayhew?" James snarled shaking his head in disbelief.

"James, just take it easy son, I want to help you. Now, put that gun down and we'll talk." Mayhew's words held no conviction.

"Not a chance on me putting this gun down. So maybe you should speak your piece and don't forget to tell me why I shouldn't kill you."

"James —"

"Shut the fuck up Yvette!" James growled.

"It's okay." Mayhew said placing a reassuring hand on Yvette's arm. "James I won't lie. You're in some real trouble. But, if you help us there's a good chance that they'll go easy on you. Dante is the one we want and you can give him to us."

"No can do." James said firmly. "I got nothing to say."

"James you're making a big mistake." Mayhew said.

"I don't think so... I'm no traitor — unlike some people," he said directing his comment at Yvette.

"James, you don't understand," Yvette said shifting feet under his rebuke. "Mayhew contacted me hoping I could help find you and talk you into helping him. We can do this James, and no matter what I'll be there for you."

"Yeah, right." James laughed. "Just like before. No, it's over between us."

"Then why did you come to this place?" Yvette asked, hurt.

"To put the past behind me." He answered flatly. "Now, as charming as this has been, I gotta go. Mayhew, you want to toss your gun in the trees?"

Slowly, Mayhew complied with James's request. Then James picked up the flashlight and pointed it at Mayhew's face. "Don't get sporty Mayhew because a man with nothing to lose is real dangerous. Goodbye, Yvette."

The light switched off and James was gone, leaving Mayhew and Yvette standing blindly in the inky darkness.

"James. James, please." Yvette pleaded to the night, but silence was her only answer.

Chapter 24

"Hope; come on baby, you gotta wake-up." James whispered, urging Hope from shock induced sleep.

Hope opened her eyes at his persistent whisper. It took her a few moments to absorb her surroundings. She found herself on a makeshift bed in what appeared to be an eight foot diameter concrete tube with capping walls about twelve feet apart. A lantern burned low above her and in the flickering light she could see graffiti and old Hair band posters on the arched walls.

"Are you okay?" His words were a soothing brush of breath against her ear.

"Where are we?" She croaked through her dry throat.

"We're in an old culvert pipe that we fixed up as a fort when we were kids. The problem is Yvette knows where it is, so we have to move. I stole a canoe so we can go down the river to the 'Griffin'." He smiled at her. "We're leaving. I washed your clothes in the spring." He set the clothes beside her. "Get dressed and I'll get you something to drink."

Hurriedly she dressed. "How long did I sleep?" She asked when he returned with a canteen.

"About twenty hours."

She looked at him thoughtfully for a moment. "Who's Yvette?"

"An old girlfriend who's working with Mayhew. Do you know him?"

"Yeah."

"Well, he's about a mile from here and Yvette's with them. I left them with no flashlight about twenty minutes ago. By the time they find their way out of the woods we should be ten or fifteen miles down river. If we get lucky they'll get lost." He took her hand "We really need to go."

James led Hope out of the huge pipe and into a stand of live oaks, it was very dark and Hope could hardly make out anything in the near complete blackness, but his step never faltered and soon they stood next to a canoe that rocked lazily on the river current. When he clicked on the flashlight to show her where to sit she wasn't surprised to see that the canoe was packed with supplies and his canvas bag of money. She climbed into the canoe as he held it steady, then, untying the mooring line, he hopped in behind her. He had instructed her to sit on the floor of the canoe and when he hopped in, she was sitting between his knees.

"You don't want me to help paddle?" She asked in a loud whisper.

"Shhh... Your voice carries. And no, I don't need your help. I'd rather have you close enough to hear me if we have to whisper."

Accepting his words she snuggled between his legs and relaxed as he rhythmically paddled constantly switching sides to keep the canoe in the center of the river. The hours drifted by slowly, but she was content to enjoy the tranquil peace in their realm of chaos. When false dawn lit the Eastern sky James expertly angled the canoe up a shallow creek. After a few hundred yards the Creek opened into a large natural spring.

"It's beautiful James." Hope said breathlessly as James nosed the canoe onto the sandy bank. "I wish we could stay here forever." Hope's voice broke slightly and tears welled up in her eyes.

"Come on now," he said soothingly, helping her from the canoe. "None of that. We're going to be okay."

"Promise?"

The question brought him up short. He couldn't lie to her and although he wanted to comfort her, he refused to make a promise he couldn't keep. How could he ever be sure of the outcome of their present situation? "I'll do my best," was all he said.

Hope picked up on his reluctance to promise her safety, but it didn't change her heart. She knew she would follow him through hell and if the end came along the way so-be-it. He was everything that she was supposed to despise – a lawless drug dealer – but James was also the only person she ever loved. The irony of her situation didn't elude her, but what was life if not a learning experience.

"How 'bout a swim," James asked stepping out of their embrace and peeling off his close with a mischievous grin.

James never ceased to amaze her. In the midst of total chaos he loved life, but that too was in complete contrast to the way he lived. He, she knew, had no inhibition of placing the life he loved, his life, in peril. In fact his very nature drove him to the edge and he thrived there with keen wit and reckless abandon. However, he sold no grand illusions and she, like everyone else, made the choice to share his destructive life. God, she thought, as she began to undress I must have lost my sanity.

When Hope dove into the lucid spring, the water was crisp and cool in the early morning heat. She swam toward James desiring the nearness of his strength, her earlier thoughts and fears washed away by the refreshing water. For what seemed a lifetime they played lovers games in the clear cool water. Then on a blanket in the sand they slept under the warmth of the midday sun...

The coolness of early evening stirred Hope from her slumber. She dressed slowly trying to shake the lingering effects of deep sleep. A short distance away James worked over an aluminum pot sitting on an open fire.

"Sleeping beauty wakes," he said as she approached him.

"Smells good. What is it?" Hope asked.

"Swamp Cabbage and rattlesnake. "You hungry?"

"Starved is more like it, but I don't know about swamp cabbage and rattlesnake."

"Give it a chance, it's not too bad if it's cooked right."

"Do I dare ask where you happen across a rattlesnake and swamp cabbage?" She asked, amused at his resourcefulness.

"Well, I was cutting the swamp cabbage when I got lucky and ran into a four foot rattlesnake."

"You call that luck?"

"Wait 'till you taste the stew," he said standing up and wrapping his arms around her. "It's good for you and you're going to need your strength; it's gonna to be a long night. We're a couple miles up the South fork of the river from Alderman Ford Park and I want to be on the other side of Lithia Springs by morning." James paused. "From there on we're going to have to be real careful."

"Why?"

"Because we'll have to start moving during the day and that means we'll be exposed." James thought for a minute before he continued. "Unless I can get us a Jon boat or something that we can act like we're fishing out of. You see, nobody canoes at night, and after we passed the springs there are a lot more houses and traffic on the river. Never mind the marine patrol, runs the river once it gets a little wider and deeper."

"Don't you know someone who would drive us to the *Griffin*?" Hope asked confused by his plan to travel by water. "I mean wouldn't that be faster?"

"Yeah it would, but Mayhew would expect that and it wouldn't surprise me if there watching my friends. Keep in mind that Yvette is with Mayhew and she knows most of my friends. Just like she knew I'd be at our place on the river." His voice trailed off.

"Do you want to talk about it?" Hope asked, sensing his pain.

"No," his voice was flat and emotionless.

"I'll never hurt you James," she said sincerely.

"Let's eat," he said in response.

~ ~ ~

"That wasn't too bad," Hope said when they were finished eating. "I didn't know you were a regular Daniel Boone."

James laughed. "I'm not. I just picked up a few tricks along the way. Come on, we need to start moving." James said pouring a pot of water on the smoldering coals.

When they were both back in the canoe James navigated the canoe down a small creek and out on the river. Night was falling and darkness was taking control of their surroundings. Hope thought about how safe she felt sitting between James' legs and how terrified she'd be if she were alone in this place at night.

Soon they passed under a roughhewn wooden bridge that seemed to appear out of nowhere. "Alderman Ford," James whispered.

Then a short time later they passed under a highway bridge, quickly followed by another wooden bridge at which point all signs of civilization vanished and the River twisted through what appeared to be untouched wilderness. Here and there they passed a dock or a shimmering light in the trees, but for the most part the night was silent and dark.

Hope had started to doze when James covered her mouth with his hand and whispered. "Be real quiet. That's Russo's car."

Hope hadn't noticed the car or the house for that matter, but she could see both clearly now...

James nosed the canoe up to the riverbank opposite the house and slipped silently out of the small boat. Soundlessly he dug through the gear packed in the nose of the canoe until he uncovered his compound bow. The razor tips of the six arrows bracketed to the bow gave an eerie reflection in the pale moonlight.

"What are you gonna do?" Hope whispered in the stillness.

Shhh." James put his mouth to Hopes ear. "Don't make a sound."

Hope shook her head in understanding.

[194]

With that, James waded into the moderate current of the river until the water was too deep to walk. Holding the bow out of the water he swam a one-hand side stroke to the far bank. Like a ghost he moved into the trees circling the house.

Silently he stood in the darkness of the trees searching the windows of the house for any sign of movement. Moments passed and the crickets began to chirp – a sure sign that nothing moved in the night.

Stealthily, James worked his way to a small metal shed and slipped silently inside. On a workbench he found the hand tools he needed to carry out his plan. Placing the tools in the pockets of his fatigues, he began to search the drawers of the workbench for a couple lengths of wire and a piece of small hose. His search was slow but meticulous and soon he had what he came for.

Again, James moved through the night but much more deliberately, crossing straight from the shed to Russo's car. Quietly he slid under the front of the Benz. Struggling into position he snaked his hand up to the battery, with a touch and feel process he found the positive connection and disconnected it. That done, he made his way to the driver side of the car trying the door handle; an evil smile crossed his features as the latch clicked...

An hour later, James swam back across the river and repacked his bow. Wordlessly he shoved the canoe off the bank and scrambled in behind Hope.

"What did you do James?" Hope asked, after they had gone a few hundred yards downstream.

"I sentenced Russo to death by fire." James felt a shiver run through Hope. "I didn't pick this fight, but I damn sure intend to win it." He said, in a way of explanation.

Chapter 25

He unceremoniously forced Trish's knees apart and entered her with a lustful pain-filled thrust.

She hated being his whore. There once was a time when she thought all men were like him, but James had shown her a tenderness and pleasure. She closed her eyes against his pox marked face and tried to ignore the pain he was inflicting on her with his rough rhythm. She knew she only had to endure his intrusion for a few minutes more and he would be satisfied at least for a while.

True to form, a couple minutes later, he shuddered, gave a grunt and crumpled down on her, withering in exhaustion.

She felt the tears well up in her eyes, but she wouldn't give this animal the satisfaction of seeing her cry. Her fear of him had kept her in his service for longer than she cared to remember and that same fear had led her to betray James, but no more.

She wiggled out from under him, slid off the bed and started for the bathroom.

"I have business this morning." Russo's voice stopped her in mid-step. "My associate has a thing for blondes, so be ready to service him when I get back."

Trish involuntarily shivered, but nodded in agreement walking into the bathroom. When she stepped into the steaming spray of the shower the dam broke and tears streamed down her face.

No, she thought, I'll do no more of his bidding, service no more of his associates, or him for that matter. She picked up the washcloth and began to scrub his sweat from her skin.

Russo dressed, thinking about the day's business. He was to meet Agent Hawthorn and make a payoff for Dante. He didn't care much for being Dante's messenger, but he needed Westhardt's connections to further his enterprise. But also, he had a plan to start his own network of corruption and Trish was the bait, at least where Hawthorn was concerned. The DEA man had expressed his desire for her at their last meeting and Russo knew how easy most men were to control by their cocks.

He smiled to himself as he retrieved his keys from the kitchen counter. Today, he thought, is the beginning of the end for Dante Westhardt. He knew that once he had his network in place he would no longer need Dante and he would give the old man a taste of real power. In all the time he'd known Dante, not one time had he seen the old man lift a finger. Instead of handling his business Dante always ordered others to do his dirty work.

Anyway, Westhardt's days were numbered the way he saw it. Dante had picked a fight with James and as confident as Russo was in himself, he had to admit that James was a formidable adversary. Twice now James had killed some of Russo's henchmen and he was secretly glad that James hadn't come for him. With any luck James would get to Dante Westhardt and solve Russo's problem for him. Russo snickered to himself – today was a good day!

Russell slid behind the wheel of his Benz and closed the door whistling a song from his childhood. He couldn't remember the words, but the melody had stayed with him over the years.

He slipped the key in the ignition and gave it a twist. The door locks clicked, giving him a start and for some reason he couldn't fathom, there was a humming coming from the doors like the sound made by the electric window motors.

"What the fuck?" He demanded as some kind of liquid began to spray him from the dash. Russo tried the door handle, frantic and confused.

The smell of gasoline quickly filled his nostrils and he looked down at the liquid that still spewed from the vents. It was that moment that he saw the kitchen match wrapped in a thin copper wire. He reached for the match and bumped his head on the steering wheel in his haste. Recovering quickly, he again reached for the match, but a second before his fingers covered the short distance, the wire turned red-hot and the match flared...

A whoosh of flame flashed and Russo was consumed in fire and searing pain. He screamed.

The bloodcurdling scream sent a cold shiver of confusion and fear through Trish. She scrambled to the bathroom window in search of the source of the scream. What she saw, when she drew the curtains, filled her with terror until the gravity of the situation set in. The interior of Russo's car was ablaze and his fiery form was clawing at the driver's window like a madman, and screaming like a banshee. For a moment, she thought about what she could do to help, but then the memory of his invasive use of her body returned. Fuck him, she thought walking back to the shower. Let the neighbors help him.

Not until the screaming stopped did it occur to Trish that someone had to be behind the fire consuming Russo.

James, she thought, and as if to confirm her thought, at that instant the car exploded, rocking the house on its foundation.

Trish wrapped herself in a terry-cloth robe and hurried to the back door. Just as she opened the door a neighbor came around the corner of the house. Showtime, she thought, crumpling down on the top step and letting go a bloodcurdling scream herself, as she forced tears to streamed down her face.

Mayhew arrived on the scene a short time later taking in the havoc in a single glance. Twisted metal and broken glass were scattered about the place, but what caught his eye were the muddy footprints leading up from the river woods.

Careful not to step on any evidence Mayhew made his way to examine the boot tracks.

Mayhew turned on his heel and began to retrace the steps.

Walking wide of the boot barks, Mayhew tracked the prints to the river's edge. After a quick glance both up and down stream, Mayhew retraced his path back to the shed and made a mental note to have the shed gone over by an evidence tech. Just in front of the shed he picked up the boot print trail that led to where the burned-out hull of the car sat. He'd seen enough.

"Who's she," Mayhew asked a uniform officer in the front yard.

"Her? She's the victim's girlfriend," the man answered, indicating the distraught woman in a terry-cloth robe. "Haven't got much out of her except her names Trish and the girlfriend fact."

"Thanks," Mayhew said over his shoulder making his way to the woman.

"Ma'am, I need to ask you a few questions," Mayhew said.

Trish nodded her head in understanding.

"Can you tell me what happened?"

"I-I w-was in," Trish intentionally stuttered smoothly as a new wave of tears rolled down her cheeks. "The shower w-when I heard a l-loud noise. I-I ran to the b-back d-door and then..." Trish chose that point to break down.

Mayhew placed a comforting hand on her shoulder. "It's okay. Just calm down." He waited for her to regain her composure. "I only have one more question ma'am. Do you know a man named Griffin James?"

Trish quickly shook her head to the negative.

~ ~ ~

Hawthorn hated to be kept waiting, most times he refused to wait, but today was different. He wanted his money, but more than that he wanted the girl.

Since the day he'd seen her in Cocoa Beach she'd haunted his thoughts, and when he'd seen her again a few days ago dancing at Russo's club he knew he had to have her. All it had taken was a simple mention of her to Dante and his wish was granted.

Now the anticipation was killing him slowly. Maybe there was something to the old adage about the thrill of the chase. Whatever it was he felt like a schoolboy, except that the outcome of this date was certain.

He was so entwined in his lustful thoughts that it took a minute for him to realize his cell phone was ringing.

"Hawthorn," he said, still fumbling with the phone.

"Hawthorn, we've got a problem," came Dante's voice through the phone. "Russo was burned alive in his car this morning."

"What?" Hawthorn exclaimed, feeling the object of his lust slip away.

"It had to be James and he has to be traveling down the river, because Mayhew and an old girlfriend encountered him there a few days ago."

"An old girlfriend? Where is she now?"

"At the Days Inn in Brandon, why?" Dante asked, perplexed.

"Because." Hawthorn said, exasperated. "Maybe I can make a trade for Hope Brooks. I mean we haven't been able to kill him, so let's try to make a deal."

"Look," Dante said flatly. "Brooks is your problem, not mine. I want James dead!"

"Well, I want to cover my ass and yours for that matter. We've been doing it your way and it hasn't worked yet, now it's my turn."

Dante didn't care much for the way Hawthorn was talking down to him, but he could deal with that later. James was all that mattered at the moment. "All right, do it," was all he said.

"What's the room number?"

"Two-eighteen."

Hawthorn bolted from the café.

Chapter 26

Hawthorn gave three sharp knocks to the door marked two-eighteen, fishing his badge out of his coat pocket at the same time.

Impatiently he tapped one foot. Time was running out on him and it was high time he took control of this disaster, before it sent him spiraling into ruin.

When the petite blonde cracked open the door, Hawthorn's badge came up with the practiced motion of a seasoned investigator. "Yvette Boyer? I'm agent Hawthorn of the DEA, I need to ask you some questions."

"All right." Yvette stumbled, unhooking the safety latch on the door.

"I'm sure you know what this is concerning," Hawthorn swung the door shut behind them. "Are you alone?"

"Yeah."

"Yeah, what?" Hawthorn asked gruffly, his impatience coming across in his voice.

"Yeah, I know what this is about and yeah I'm alone," Yvette's answer was just as sharp as his question.

She hated pushy people and of the past two days of worrying about James had her wits on end.

"Does James know anyone along the river between Lithia Springs and Bell Shoels Road?"

"Not that I know of." Yvette answered. "But we haven't been a serious item in years and James knows people everywhere."

Hawthorn pondered her answer for a moment deciding on his next course of action. "If we can find him do you think you could talk him into giving himself up?"

"I doubt it," she answered with a snort of disbelief. "But I'll surely try. I don't want James to die like his father and grandfather."

"And how was that?" Hawthorn asked, playing the role. Dante had already told him the story and he doubted that James even knew the whole story. Dante had confessed his involvement in both shootings to Hawthorn, and if Dante had his way he would see that the last heir to the James family legacy met his fate.

"At the hands of the police," Yvette answered coldly.

"I'm on your side ma'am," Hawthorn lied.

~ ~ ~

The midday sun pushed it sweltering heat through the canopy of the trees, but James seemed not to notice, as he kept up an exhausting tempo paddling the canoe.

Hope, for the most of the morning, was content to ride between James' legs in silence, watching the birds fly to and fro, or studying the occasional house they passed.

James too, studied their surroundings. However, nature was not the subject of his scrutiny. His eyes searched out the unnatural movement as his ears strained to hear the unnatural sound. Yet, all seemed normal, almost to a fault.

James' stomach churned forebodingly with every stroke of his paddle, and he couldn't help but think that every breath brought him one closer to his last. Something was coming his way; he could feel it and whatever it was, it damn sure wasn't good. He wondered in dread if Hope could feel it also, but said nothing.

He had long tired of the situation he placed himself in more than a year ago and his earlier regret of murdering Warren forced its way to the forefront of his mind. Quickly the weight of his decision to attack Dante's house fell on his conscious and he silently mourned the loss of his friends. Their fate too, was on his hands. Although he could not have imagined the outcome, they lost their lives because of yet another poor choice he'd made.

"What are you thinking about?" Hope turned slightly to look up at him.

James hadn't realized that he'd stopped paddling. "I was just thinking how glad I'd be when we're back on the *Griffin* and out to sea." His words weren't a complete lie. In his heart, for the first time in his life he wanted to be anywhere, but his beloved river. He kissed her forehead and began to paddle again.

~ ~ ~

Hawthorn and Yvette sat in Hawthorn's unmarked government car parked at the shoulder of the Bell Shoels Road bridge.

Hawthorn's gaze was fixed – as it had been for hours – on the slight bend in the river eighty yards upstream from the bridge. His eyes swam in and out of focus as he constantly searched for any signs of movement.

Yvette, however, was too tormented by her thoughts to concentrate on the river. She couldn't help but blame herself for the road James chose. Maybe she could have been the factor that led James to lead a normal life. Instead, she had abandoned the young love, a strong love, and even though he'd come to her many times in the months since their reunion, they'd never regained what they once had.

"They're coming! Let's move!" Hawthorn insisted, scrambling from the car.

James saw the sudden movement of two people hurrying onto the bridge and stopped his rhythmic paddling, letting the canoe drift on the lazy current. Instantly his own awareness went on Red Alert slowing the world down to still frames clicking past.

James felt Hope tense between his legs. "That's Hawthorn, my boss," she whispered.

"And Yvette, my ex." James added.

What happened next took both by surprise.

When Hawthorn and Yvette reached the middle of the bridge Hawthorn pulled his pistol and pointed it to Yvette's head. James and Hope watched in shock horror as Hawthorn handcuffed Yvette behind her back and shoved her against the guardrail.

"James," Hawthorn shouted. "It's *Let's Make a Deal* time!"

The canoe was drifting ever closer to the bridge, but the distance was still too great for James to read the expression on Hawthorn's face.

"Speak your piece." James shot back in answer.

"I propose a trade. Yvette here," Hawthorn shoved Yvette farther over the guardrail to emphasize his point, "for Brooks."

"He wants to kill you," James whispered matter-of-factly, but only loud enough for Hope's ears. Then he shouted, "What if I don't like the trade?"

"Then I push her over the side and take my chance with this." Hawthorn held up his pistol and gave it a shake.

They had drifted close enough now that James could see the frustration on the other man's face.

The seconds ticked by.

"Please James!" Yvette pleaded.

"What's it gonna be?" Hawthorn questioned inpatient now.

"Save Yvette," James whispered to Hope. He raised his voice "Hawthorn!"

"Yeah."

"Fuck you!" James saw the flash of anger cross Hawthorn's features.

Hope drew a quick surprised breath and watched in defenseless horror as Hawthorn pushed Yvette over the rail.

While Yvette tumbled through the air, Hawthorn leveled his weapon on James and Hope, but just before he squeezed the trigger, James intentionally turned the canoe over – spilling himself, Hope, and their gear into the murky water.

The suddenness with which James flipped the canoe took Hope by surprise, but as she hit the water, James' earlier words came back to her *save Yvette*.

[204]

Hope dove for the bottom and swam for the bridge to search for Yvette.

James swam straight for the bottom and searched the dark water for their slowly sinking gear. He found the tent first and quickly discarded it.

His lungs began to burn and he hastened his pace.

Yvette plunged into the water in stark terror and shocked disbelief. James had forsaken her. She kicked wildly in a futile attempt to reach the surface.

Hawthorn had taken to quick shots before he regained his senses and reasoned that they had to come up for air. He waited.

James, in dire need of oxygen, found the bag of gear for which he'd been searching. He went perfectly still in the water until he felt the push of the river current and swam downstream...

Hope resurfaced just a few feet from the cover of the bridge, a mistake that almost cost her, her life. Almost immediately, a bullet passed by her face so close she felt the displacement of air.

She gulped a breath and disappeared into the depths of the murky river as a hail of hollow points tore through the water around her.

Ironically enough it was Hawthorn's rash hail storm of bullets that enabled Hope to find Yvette. In her thrashing attempt to escape Hawthorn's attack, Hope collided with Yvette's body in the dark depths of the river.

Hope grabbed a handful of Yvette's shirt and swam for the surface, careful to come up under the protection of the bridge.

James surfaced in the shallows fifty feet from where Hope held Yvette's limp body against a pylon near the center of the river. "Is she okay?" James called out to Hope, as he freed his compound bow from its canvas bag.

"James," Hope said in desperation, whipping her head around to face him. "She's not breathing..."

Before James could react to Hopes' words a bullet knocked a chunk of concrete off the pylon close to him and he dropped back into the water. He knew instinctively that the shot had come from the far side of the river. With that in mind he drifted with the current to change his position and at the same time popped an arrow from the rack on his bow.

When he stood up in the chest deep water, bow drawn, arrow ready, he quickly found Hawthorn on the far bank. Without hesitation he let the arrow fly. In his haste he hadn't lifted the bow completely out of the water and his shot suffered because of the friction.

Hawthorn squeezed off a single shot before James disappeared again. "Brooks," he yelled and frustration. "You've gotten yourself in real trouble! But if you give up I might be able to help you."

Hope had the pylon between herself and Hawthorn, but her muscles were beginning to cramp from holding Yvette against the structure and she knew time was running out because Yvette was starting to turn blue from lack of oxygen. Where was James?

He swam upstream with the bow held against his chest until he saw the sun, indicating he was no longer under the bridge. As he swam for the far side he thought about Yvette. Hope had said she wasn't breathing and that meant time was on Hawthorn's side. His next attempt, James knew, had to be successful or Yvette would be dead, and he couldn't bear to lose another friend due to poor choice on his part.

When he reached the shallows on the opposite side of the river, he freed another arrow from the rack. The shot would not be an easy one, he knew, because he had to turn the bow sideways in an effort to avoid his earlier mistake.

With a confidence he didn't feel he spring through the surface and instantly located Hawthorn thirty feet away.

Hawthorn turned to face the sudden commotion bringing his pistol around to mount an attack. But just as he squared his shoulders for a shot the arrow ripped through his left chest and out his back.

James saw the confusion in Hawthorn's eyes and then confusion turned to realization as death took control.

Hawthorn crumpled to a heap.

Chapter 27

Hope helped James carry Yvette's listless body to the riverbank, where they lay her in the thick grass.

Hope positioned herself and performed CPR but James stopped her. "We have to get the cuffs off first."

He scanned their surroundings for discarded trash.

James held up a silencing hand in answer and jogged over to a beer can at the base of a bridge. He used his pocket knife to cut a thin strip off the can as he returned to Hope and said. "Turn her on her side."

Hope wasted no time obeying his instruction. If she had learned one thing from James, it was the fact that he knew his limitations. Hope watched in amazement as James expertly slipped the thin shim from the can under the gear of the cuffs and released Yvette's right hand.

In a controlled frenzy, James positioned Yvette for CPR, automatically Hope went to her knees and began pumping Yvette's chest. After a five count James pinched Yvette's nose closed and blew a sharp breath into her mouth.

Again, hope began pumping.

"Come on, Yvette." James whispered, silently counting Hope's pumps. Desperately he blew his life's breath into Yvette's lungs watching her chest rise and fall, but still she showed no sign of recovery.

"Don't give up, James." Hope encouraged, starting her compressions again.

James closed his eyes and willed Hope all his strength. Too many people had died because of his poor decisions. How could he lose Yvette and not his sanity? He placed his mouth to hers and released another sharp breath into her lungs...

Yvette coughed up the river water in her lungs and drew a quick short choking breath.

James gathered Yvette in his arms, holding her as she struggled to regain a normal breathing rhythm.

"Go to Hawthorn's car and radio an ambulance," James said to Hope. "But come right back."

"You saved me, James." Yvette said as soon as she could speak.

"No," he said. "Hope saved you."

"Hope?"

"It's a long story."

When Hope returned James told her to stay with Yvette, then he swam out to where he'd turned the canoe over and dove for the bottom as Hope and Yvette looked on in confusion. After a few moments he came up for air ten yards from where he went down but he was gone again before Hope could holler for him to explain his actions.

When he next appeared he came walking out of the water, the weight of a canvas bag holding him to the bottom of the river.

"What are you doing?" Hope demanded.

"Getting my money," James said, cocking his head to the distant sound of sirens. "And I'm running out of time."

He dove back in the river to continue his search. James knew the sirens were coming to Yvettes aid, and he knew he needed not be here when they arrived. But if he was going to make a life with Hope he needed the money. Desperately he searched the murky water for the second bag, his lungs burning their desire for oxygen into his chest. He was about to give up his search — faced with the knowledge that his time had run out — when he happened to come across the other bag of cash.

In need of air and out of time, James dragged the other bag from the river, only to find that Hope had driven Hawthorn's car down the bridge slope and close to the bank.

The sirens blared, far too close for comfort. James struggled with the considerable weight of the canvas bags of wet money, loading them into the backseat of Hawthorn's car. When that was done he opened one bag and grabbed three thick stacks of hundred dollar bills. Yvette watched him, still confused as he closed the short distance between the car and where she sat in the grass.

"Take this," James said kneeling beside her and laying the stacks in her lap.

"I don't want your money, James," Yvette grumbled in the strongest voice she could muster. "I want you."

James turned his head and drew a deep breath through his nostrils, with Hope looking on. "I've gotta go," he whispered, brushing a kiss on Yvette's cheek. "This is goodbye." A tear slipped down his face as he took Hope's hand and led her to the waiting car.

The dust that James and Hope had left in their wake hadn't settled when the ambulance arrived.

~ ~ ~

Mayhew couldn't believe the transformation in Yvette since he'd last seen her. Her hollow defeated appearance brought him up short and he took a moment to gather himself before approaching the tormented young woman.

He'd been on-scene for ten minutes and the mystery of several cases on his slate were beginning to unfold. He had no doubt that James was behind the murder of Hawthorn, and Russo for that matter. However, more than a few things didn't add up. Why had Hawthorn come here without backup? Why bring Yvette? And where did Russo figure into this tangle of death and destruction? It was those answers he hoped to get from Yvette.

"Are you okay?" He asked disarmingly as he approached her.

Yvette turned away, choosing not to answer.

"Yvette, please, I need your help."

"Why? So y'all can kill James!" She snarled at him. "Fuck you!"

This is going to be more difficult than Mayhew had thought. How could he blame her, though? He tried a different approach. "Can you at least tell me what happened here?"

"Yeah," she shouted in anger. "Your buddy tried to drown me and James killed him while his girlfriend, Hope, save me."

So Brooks is still with James, Mayhew thought. Now he had to figure out where they were going.

"How is it that you and agent Hawthorn ended up here?"

"That bastard came to my room and got me, that's how."

"What happened when you got here?"

"We waited for James and when he came down the river your buddy tried to trade me for James' girlfriend. When James refused, your asshole buddy pushed me off the bridge, handcuffed behind my back." Yvette said visibly calming.

At her words Mayhew was becoming angry. If she was telling the truth Hawthorn was dirty. Why would she lie? And if Hawthorn was dirty that would explain a lot of the mysteries? What now? He took a shot in the dark. "Why didn't you go with James?"

"Because," Yvette spat her words. "He's got that bitch with him."

Now he was getting someplace. All he had to do was figure out why James had stayed on the river and where he was going. "Does James have any friends down river that you know of?"

"You're starting to sound like your buddy over there." Yvette pointed to Hawthorn's body on the other side of the river. "And I'll tell you the same thing I told him, James knows everybody. But if he knows someone down river, I've never met them."

"Why stick to the river then?" Mayhew was thinking out loud more than asking a question, but he was rewarded just the same.

"His boat is probably down-stream." Yvette said.

"His boat?"

"Yeah, he bought a big boat in West Palm. We spent a couple days on it right after he bought it."

"Do you know the name of the boat?" Mayhew asked, thankful for the break.

"Yeah, he named it the *Griffin*. I made a joke 'cause he hates his name."

"Stay with her," Mayhew told a nearby uniform. "No one and I mean no one talks to her until further notice."

"Gotcha," the uniform answered as Mayhew jogged off.

Chapter 28

The dock attendant gave James a suspicious look when he settled his slip fees and fuel bill with a wad of wet hundred dollar bills, but James was far too preoccupied to notice.

He left the office and started down the dock where Hope waited by the *Griffin*. Closing the distance between them, James, thought about how their lives had crashed together, and too, he marveled at how two people from different worlds could find each other in the midst of chaos. In the short time they'd spent together Hope had taught James to love again and the realization caused him to miss a step.

Strange, James thought, the way love found you, but what did it matter now? He had the money. He had the boat. And he had Hope; nothing else mattered. He wrapped his arms around her and kissed her forehead.

"I love you," he whispered, surprised by the truth of his words.

"I love you too."

For a long minute they shared the moment and tears welled up in Hope's eyes as the tension in her muscles dissipated. They had, against all odds, made it, and now they had each other as well as the rest of their lives to share.

"Let's go." James mood visibly lightening as he untied the mooring lines. "Paradise waits."

"Where are we going?" Hope asked following James up the external stairs to the control bridge.

"Any place you want to," he answered, bringing the powerful motors of the yacht rumbling to life. "So long as it's not a territory of the United States." He shot a glance at Hope. "You understand that we can't come back don't you?"

Hope considered his words and she did understand the magnitude of their meaning. "Will you promise me something, then?"

"What's that?"

She sat in his lap and stared into his eyes. "You'll stay with me forever?"

James saw something unspoken move behind her eyes, but he couldn't put his finger on it. "Loyalty has its rewards and I'm your prize," he said jokingly.

"I'm serious, James."

"I am too." The hint of laughter gone from his voice now. "You don't really know me that well yet, but you'll see that I don't swear my loyalty easily and when I do I never betray it. When I said I love you that was an oath of my loyalty and I'd died before I'd forsake that."

Hope snuggled down in his lap and for the first time in her life knew what the words *true love* meant. She'd known from that first night, when James saved her, that she loved this man and now the knowledge that he shared her emotion seemed to justify the decisions she made along the way. Life as she knew it, was over, but this was the beginning of a new life, a happier life.

James navigated the *Griffin* through the mouth of the river and into the bay turning toward the Sunshine Skyway Bridge and the open waters of the Gulf of Mexico. Soon they would be in International Waters and free forever from the evil that had changed their lives.

~ ~ ~

"Dispatch, this is homicide detective Mayhew."

"Copy for Mayhew." Came a metallic voice as Mayhew turned West on Balm Boyette Road and stabbed the accelerator of his Crown Vic to the floorboard.

"I need every available person to start calling the boat slips on the Alifia River searching for a boat called the *Griffin*. Copy?"

"Copy. A boat called *Griffin*?"

"Copy. And get the Captain online; I need to talk to him ASAP."

"The Captain?"

"Captain Green," Mayhew shouted into the mic. "Tell him I'm in pursuit of a multiple murder suspect so it's kind of important."

"Copy."

"Fuck," Mayhew swore out loud, narrowly missing an oncoming car as he slid onto Riverview Drive. No sooner than he had regained control of the car an old woman pulled out in front of him and he had to slam the brakes to avoid hitting her. "God-dammit," he screamed, "they will be out to sea before I get there."

He grabbed up the mic. "Dispatch. Mayhew."

"Go for Mayhew."

"I want the helicopter in the air now! Destination Riverview. Copy?"

"Copy. Destination Riverview?"

"Yeah... Yeah. Where's the goddamn Captain?"

"We tried his cell. No answer. We paged him. Copy?"

"Copy. Did you find the boat?"

"Negative. We'll contact you as soon as we have the requested info."

"Well, make it snappy would ya? Mayhew out."

Mayhew whipped his car to the shoulder of the road and past the old woman on the right. He shot a glance at the woman as he drew even with her and to his surprise she was giving him the finger as he sped by. What, he thought, is the world coming to?

Mayhew was waiting on a red light when the radio cracked again. "Dispatch to Mayhew. We have a boat named the *Griffin*, but according to the slip manager it pulled out about twenty minutes ago."

Mayhew smashed the wheel with the palm of his hand. "From where?" He said angrily into the mic.

"From Highway 41, in Gibsontin."

"Where's that god-damn helicopter I asked for?"

"Right above you, sir," came a different metallic voice from the speaker.

"Stay with me, until I can find an LZ" Mayhew said more calmly.

"Roger that."

Mayhew turned right on Highway 301 and raced north, whipping in and out of traffic like a madman with a death wish. When at last he reached the on ramp for the expressway his nerves were a frazzled mess. He launched the car into the median and brought it to a lurching halt. By the time he scrambled from the car the helicopter was landing a few yards away.

"Fly for the Skyway Bridge," he yelled over the thumping sound of the rotors as he climbed into the vacated copilots seat and slipped on the headgear.

"Roger that..."

~ ~ ~

James turned the *Griffin* into the shipping channel and bumped the throttles up to three quarters full causing a tremble of power to shudder through the yacht's hull as it gained speed.

Soon they would pass under the Sunshine Skyway and into the Gulf of Mexico, and on to freedom.

He reached out and took Hope's hand giving it a gentle squeeze. "Where do you want to go?"

"How 'bout Hell?" Came a husky voice from the inner stairwell.

In perfect unison Hope and James twisted toward the voice, but James need not see the intruders face; he knew the voice all too well. James began to slowly work his knife out of his pocket.

"I guess you're being here means your fresh out of henchmen?" James said with confidence he didn't feel.

"You've proven to be quite the adversary," the intruder said, "but the game's over and it looks as though you lose." The intruder leveled his semi-automatic handgun at James' head.

"I didn't start this war," James said, stalling for time.

"You don't know the half of it." Dante laughed. "This war has been raging quietly for more than sixty years, but it's over today. Today I see the last member of the James family die and rightfully so. You see, my daddy was there the night your grandfather was shot down, and years later I saw your father meet the same fate."

James involuntarily cringed while Hope watched and listened slack-jawed.

"My daddy," Dante continued, "always said *the apple don't fall far from the tree* and he was right. Every goddamn one of you James' thought you could defy the Westhardts and in the end we've proven each one of you wrong."

Something caught Dante's attention and for a split second his eyes shifted to the external door, that was the break James was waiting for. Like a snake coiled to strike, James spring from his chair. Working with the thumb lock to snap opened the blade of his knife, he made an underhand, midair throw, as he crashed into Hope driving her from her seat and landing protectively on her.

A shot rang out and James flinched but the round had harmlessly passed through the windshield. Then over the ringing in his ears he heard the dull thud of a body hitting the floor. James dared a glance over his shoulder and found Dante's writhing body in its final death row, blood gurgling around the handle of the knife buried in his throat.

"Is he dead?" Hope asked in a panting whisper.

"Close enough," James answered remorselessly.

James helped Hope to her feet and pulled her close as he shoved the throttles to full speed ahead and righted the vessel's course.

"Back those throttles down and turn around real slow," came a voice from the external doorway. "I have a gun pointed at you."

This time it was Hope who knew the face that went with the voice. "Captain Green," she said in confusion as she turned to face him. "What are you doing here?"

[217]

"You're a smart girl. Figure it out." The Captain glanced at James. "Your boyfriend here, has undermined my plans at every turn and single-handedly undone a network that I've been building for forty years." Pure evil danced in the captain's eyes. "Now I've got to cut my losses and clean up the mess. The only plus to this whole mess is that your boyfriend has managed to kill everyone involved while eluding death himself."

"Are you saying you're responsible for the deaths of all these murderers we attributed to Dante Westhardt?" Hope stalling now.

"Let's just say that Dante Westhardt and I go way back and for more years than either of you have been alive, Dante has paid me to ensure that he could operate his drug trade without hindrance from the Sheriff's Office."

"And Hawthorn?" Hope asked, completely dumbfounded.

"On the payroll, too." The captain waved his pistol. "Now who's first?"

"Why not just let us leave?" James asked, positioning himself slightly ahead and to one side of Hope.

"No can do," the captain said flatly.

~ ~ ~

Mayhew searched the open waters of the bay for any sign of the *Griffin*, but to no avail. They had flown straight to the Skyway Bridge and were now sweeping the bay east to west in a back-tracking course, Mayhew searched the distant horizon with binoculars for any sign of the yacht.

Mayhew knew that by all logical reason they should have James trapped in the bay, but a foreboding premonition was growing in his stomach – time was running out... Perspiration broke out and gathered in large drops on his forehead, then dripped off his brow into his eyes. Mayhew pulled the binoculars away and wiped his eyes on his sleeve.

[218]

With his heart hammering in expectation, Mayhew brought the binoculars back to his eyes. Slowly he swung his head right and left searching the distance for any sign of movement. When a large vessel came into view on the west side of the bay his heart rate involuntarily doubled as he pointed the boat out to the pilot.

The nose of the chopper dipped and the machine accelerated with a sickening lunge. Quickly the distance shrink until only a few hundred yards separated the flying machine and the yacht.

"Bring us in close and at the stern," Mayhew said into the radio.

Instantly the pilot put the helicopter into a sweeping dive as Mayhew searched the vessel for any indication of who was on board. When the stern of the hull came into view Mayhew silently read the name stenciled there – Southern Belle – "Wrong boat," he said in frustration as the yacht captain scrambled out on the deck.

The helicopter banked right and began to regain altitude all the while Mayhew's foreboding feeling growing at an alarming rate.

~ ~ ~

"There's around two million dollars in those bags." James pointed to the duffel bags in the corner of the room. "Why not take the money for our freedom?"

"That's no bargain," Captain Green said. "In case you haven't noticed I've got the gun and after I take care of you two I still get the money, with no strings."

The helicopter was nearly on top of them before they heard it. In unison all shifted their focus toward the unexpected sound.

The Captain saw first the sniper positioned in the side door, then Mayhew in the copilot seat. He should have known. He growled in anger as he felt his stranglehold on this situation slipping away. Fire raged in his heart and in his eyes. He spun on his heel and brought the sites of his pistol to rest on Hope – kill the bitch – he thought, before it's too late.

James saw the sudden change in the Captain's demeanor and the intent in his eyes. Without a second thought he dove in front of Hope, a millisecond later the sound of the Captains pistol came in an ear shattering roar.

James felt the round tear into his left chest breaking ribs and shredding flesh as it penetrated. The world swam out of focus as he crashed to the floor.

Mayhew, who had been completely baffled when he saw his Captain on the *Griffin* was quickly gaining understanding. Why was the Captain here? There could only be one reason and why had he attempted to kill a Federal Agent? Again only one reason. The Captain had to be dirty.

"Take out Captain Green," Mayhew said to the sniper.

"I can't shoot the Captain," the sniper said in shocked disbelief.

"Then give me the goddamn rifle." Mayhew snatched the weapon from the stunned man.

It had been some time since Mayhew had handled a rifle, but he was surprised how comfortable it felt in his hands. Without hesitation he shoved the barrel of the weapon through the small sliding window of the copilot door and sighted the crosshairs of the scope on the Captain's back.

Hope watched in horror as the Captain closed the distance between himself and where she sat with a dying James in her lap. The captain stopped a few feet from her and began to raise his pistol. Hope drew, what she was sure was her last breath...

Hope heard a sharp crack and to her amazement the Captain jerked violently to his left, contorted unnaturally and crumpled to the floor. Hope expelled her breath as tears streamed down her face.

"Don't cry," James said, a pink froth coming out of his mouth. "It's over." He gasped in pain. "And our secret dies with me."

"You can't die, James," hope pleaded. "Please don't die, I'm pregnant."

James' eyes flared open, *the curse lives*, he thought. "I love you Hope," he whispered as his body wracked in spasms of pain. "Don't let our son die like me."

Hope screamed in anguish as James went slack in her arms.

The End

RJ BUCHANAN

From the author:

I chose a work of fiction because you'd never believe the truth. In a world where self-gratification and violence rule the 'Game' the truth is often unbelievable!

Take it from someone who was there.

sincerly,

Ralph Buchanan

RJBUCHANAN1970@GMAIL.COM

Made in the USA
Columbia, SC
21 February 2021

33301141R10124